GOD'S FAILURES

BY THE SAME AUTHOR.

LIFE IN ARCADIA (Arcady Library). Cr. 8vo. 5*s. net.* With Illustrations by PATTEN WILSON.

A pleasanter book it would be hard to find amongst recent literature.'—*The Speaker.*

'A work which only a writer of genuine imagination could produce.'—*Publisher's Circular.*

THE WONDERFUL WAPENTAKE. Cr. 8vo. 5*s.* 6*d. net.* With Illustrations by J. AYTON SYMINGTON.

Mr. Fletcher has, in these delightful sketches of rural life, proved himself no unworthy successor of Jefferies.'—*Whitehall Review.*

'A book to reserve for one's quietest and best moments. The author is a lover of Nature, and has studied her moods as sympathetically as ever the late Richard Jefferies did.'—*The Star.*

BALLADS OF REVOLT. Sq. 32mo. 2*s.* 6*d. net.*

LONDON: JOHN LANE, THE BODLEY HEAD

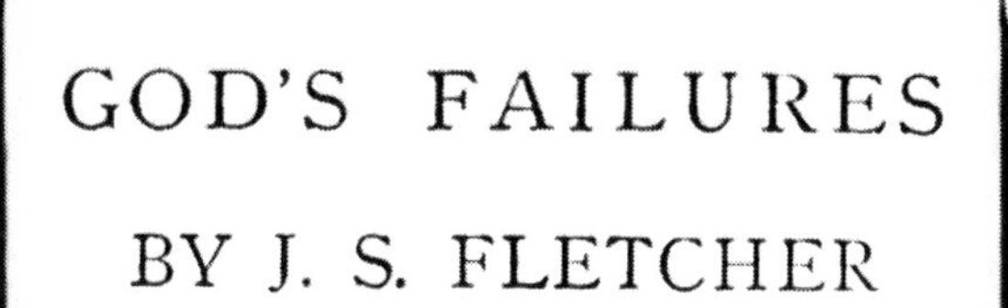

GOD'S FAILURES

BY J. S. FLETCHER

JOHN LANE: *The Bodley Head*
LONDON AND NEW YORK. 1897

TO

MY DEAR WIFE

CONTENTS

LIGHT O' LOVE

THERE suddenly came upon her, as she stood in the glare and horror of the London midnight, an intense longing to go back to the little village. For a moment she closed her eyes to the glitter of the lamps, her ears to the jests and blasphemies of the mob that surged about her. Again, as in a dream, she heard the birds singing and chirping in the garden gay with apple-blossom; again, as in a rare vision, she saw the low hills wrapped in the blue-grey mist of early morning, and beneath them the winding stream that girt the village as with a silver belt. She smelt the smell of the fields, the divine fragrance of the brown soil turned up by the glittering ploughshare, the scent of leaves that lie thick and heavy in wood and lane when autumn comes, the perfume of new-made hay, the odour of grass and hedgerow when the April showers have fallen upon them. And through all she caught the sound of village bells—chiming, chiming, chiming.

She opened her eyes and looked around her. Strange to dream so in that foul corner of the world! All that she saw there was of hell—not of the blessed earth that God made and smiled upon. And she? With a sudden gesture of impatient powerlessness she shook her head and moved away. The crowd of unholy revellers swallowed her up into itself, and the lamps glittered over it and shut out the silent stars.

But the next day she went back. The longing was irresistible—it would not be denied. Home she must go—she must see once more the familiar places and the familiar faces too, even if it cost her—what? What could it cost her that was worth the giving? She had naught to give, for she was no longer, even in her own mind, the possessor of anything that is worth possession. She was the outcast of the world—and yet there remained within her more than one fine feeling that cried from soul to body for mercy, for opportunity to breathe and to live. Not altogether had body killed soul in her, and it was the soul, weak, and perhaps all the mightier because of its weakness, that now sent her back in search of what she knew quite well she would never find again.

The village looked just the same, as she drew near to its tall elms and grey church spire. It was October, and a grey day; there was a misty softness in the air that seemed to her strikingly familiar. She gazed and gazed, and could have gazed again and for ever, at each well-known scene and object. She counted the elms that made a long avenue at the entrance to the village. There used to be four-and-twenty of them; now there were only twenty-two—the wind or the lightning had destroyed two of them. And there was the carpenter's shop, and the men busied at the benches; and here in its nook in the hedgerow was the well whereat she had drunk a thousand times. So with all things along the village street. It was mid-afternoon, and the men were at work in the fields, and the children's voices came like the hum of a beehive from the little school. Only the women were at home, and they sat by the stick fires, sewing, knitting, gossiping. In all the long, wide street she saw no face either of friend or stranger. But once or twice she peeped timidly through the little windows, and saw old faces by the hearth, the white-frilled caps making specks of light against the shadows. How peaceful it all was! How full of quiet charm!

And then in her soul rose up the picture of that other life in the foul city.

At the door of a lonely cottage just outside the village she knocked timidly. A woman answered her knock, and stood with one hand on the latch looking at the stranger. She was a stolid-faced, unimpressionable woman, plainly clad, but clean and neat of person. The woman at the door looked back at her, and was full of curious envy.

'Martha!'

The woman within the cottage started.

'Well!' she said, 'did ye iver see! Why, it's Poppy! Come in wi' you, lass—come in, and sit yoursen down.'

She walked in and sat down, and looked about her with eyes from which that curious envy and regret had not yet faded. There was a cradle by the fire, and she bent over it.

'Yours?' she whispered.

'Ay, lass, for sure. We 've had nine on 'em, and they 're all alive but one. There 's been a deal to do wi' 'em,' said Martha meditatively, 'but I don't know if I should like to loise one on 'em. And what brings you here, lass? I thowt we 'd lost all sight on you.'

'I couldn't rest, Martha,' she answered. 'I couldn't. I felt that I must come and look at the old place again. And so I came—it 's so little changed,' she said pathetically.

'Nay, there 's none so much change about it,' said Martha. 'T' change is all wi' t' men and women — t' owd spots change hardly onny. Ye 'll be livin' i' London, then?' she asked.

'Yes, I am living in London, Martha.'

'Are ye wed, lass?'

'No.'

Martha looked round the kitchen as if she feared an eavesdropper.

'Theer wor some varry queer tales about ye, lass,' she said, not unkindly. 'Ay, I don't know what mak' theer wor'rnt. But I niver took no notice on 'em—ye were a good lass enow i' t' owd days, and I allus respected your poor uncle and aunt—ha' ye been to see their graves, lass?'

'No, Martha, no!—but I will. Oh, I wish I'd never left home!—why did I? But there, what's the good of that?' She began to laugh almost hysterically. 'Come, Martha, don't let's be dowly now that I've come to see the old spot. See, I'm rich—look at my purse! You tell me all your news, and I'll tell you about London, and we'll have a good old talk.'

Martha looked at her curiously.

'Ay, well, lass,' she said, 'I'll mak' a cup o' tea—it'll do you no harm. An owd face is welcome here—not 'at yours is an owd face, for it's young enow and pretty enow.'

Poppy's lips tightened.

'Don't talk about me,' she said. 'Tell me about the old place. Who's got my uncle's farm, and is old John dead, and where has David gone?—come, tell me all about it, Martha.'

So they sat and talked while the afternoon drew on to night. In the twilight Martha's husband came home, and with him the children who had spent the day at school. Poppy sat and watched them—and in her heart grew up a great envy of Martha's lot.

A great restlessness came over her. She left

the cottage, saying that she would go for a walk in the village, and return early. So she passed down the winding lane towards the four cross-roads, whose meeting made a centre in the village street. Now and then a homeward-bound labourer passed her in the darkness, and gave her a civil good-night. The gloom refreshed her—it seemed to her that for years and years she had walked in a blinding glare that had scorched heart and brain. There had never been such refreshing gloom as this mystic twilight that lingered under the dripping elm-trees.

She reached the street. There was a bright light behind the red blinds of the 'King William,' and from a door opposite came a gleam of still brighter light across the highway. Into this door young folks were passing; a knot of young men and lads stood near it; it seemed plain that some event was about to take place within the room inside. She remembered that room and the cranky stairway that led to it. It was there that they used to hold dances and village festivities in the old days that she so regretted. Could it be that there was to be a dance there that night? She turned to a man smoking his pipe in the angle of a wall close by, and made inquiry of him. It was a dance—old Tommy was going to play the fiddle for them—there he was, going in now, and the fiddle was under his arm, wrapped in a pillow-case.

A flood of memories came over her as she stood gazing at the door, and they crowded thicker and faster as the scrape, scrape, scrape of the fiddle squeaked its way down the rickety stairs. From her place in the gloom she saw young men and women, once her companions and playmates, trooping up the stairs. There was plenty of high-voiced laughter and rude merrymaking amongst them, and the sound of it smote her like the knots of a whip. And in the smart and agony of it something prompted her to forget everything and to go in and dance and make merry as in the old, dead times. Why not?—they knew nothing; it was only she herself that knew.

She ran across the highway, and darted upstairs. She laughed gaily—it was just in that light-hearted fashion that she used to run out of the old farmhouse to the dance in the past. Why, the past was living again! She laughed once more to think of it. Gone were the evil days—she was a child, innocent and secretless, again—and there was the jolly old fiddler scraping away at his dear old fiddle.

The long low room was full of blazing light from a hundred lamps and candles. They were pairing off for the first dance as she burst in upon them, and she knew instantly that every man and every woman paused and stood and looked at her. But she heeded, or made believe that she heeded, nothing. There was nobody that she did not know, and she made for the first group, and hailed them as if all were as it once had been.

'Why, Letty, Nell, Mary, this is fun! To think that you should be having a dance the very day of my return! It's like old times—I haven't had a real good country dance I don't know when. Come, where is there a partner? Ah, Dick, you and I have danced together many a time—you shall dance this with me. Why, you and I were sweethearts in the old days, Dick. Come—come along—your arm, sir—the old fiddle's as squeaky as ever, isn't it, Dick?'

The man whom she addressed stared at

her wonderingly; the girls shrank away from her. She saw or seemed to see nothing; she put her hand on the man's arm. He, unwilling, mesmerised as it appeared by her presence, began to dance with her, looking appealingly at his companions as she led him away. There was talking, whispering, nodding of heads—she saw nothing. Her eyes were bright, there was real colour in her cheeks, her tongue rattled volubly to the astonished man who held her mechanically.

A girl ran down the steps and across the road to Dick's house. Dick's wife, arrayed in festival attire, met her at the door.

'I 'm a bit late, lass,' she said, and then stopped. 'What 's t' matter?'

The girl, excited to breathlessness by her great news, panted rather than spoke.

'There 's Poppy Mallet come back — and she 's a-dancin' wi' your Dick!'

Dick's wife stared and comprehended, and marched across the road. She walked up the stairs and into the dancing-room. Some of the young men and women, the more careless, had begun to dance, but the greater part of the floor space was left to Dick and Poppy.

'Out!'

The fiddle stopped with a screech; the floor, innocent of wax, re-echoed the thud with which each couple brought its gyrations to an end; every man and woman drew towards the centre of the floor. There stood Poppy, torn from Dick's encircling arm; there stood Dick, frightened and abashed; there, too, stood Dick's wife, one finger stretched in eloquent indignation towards the girl.

'Out you go!' she cried. 'Out! out! out! I say.'

The other woman turned and looked about her. Every face was known to her, but in none did she see a sign of pity or of friendliness. The men looked at each other, at their boots, at the wall; the women stared straight and stonily at herself. She looked at them once, twice, and then she turned and left the room without a word.

The news had spread. At the door and in the road the older women of the village had assembled, full of indignation and resentment. She heard the murmurs that broke out at sight of her, and took no heed of them. She went up the road and into the darkness, and disappeared, and the group of observers melted and talked of her.

A mile away along the road she turned across the moorland. Her feet stumbled over the rough ground, but she kept on, brushing the darkness from her with hands that trembled. The moon was rising somewhere in the heavens, and the landscape grew lighter moment by moment. She saw a tree start out of the darkness, and remembered it, and turned away in another direction. For a long time she walked steadily on, but at last she paused, and looked up to the sky, and waited. Suddenly the white moon shot out from a deep cloud-bank, and showed her the edge of the cliff, and beneath it, far down in the ravine, the jagged edges of the rocks that hemmed in the howling river.

THE LAST OF THE DRINGS

I

NOT even the most learned of local historians could put his finger on any one of the years that have followed each other since the Norman came, and say with certainty, 'At this time there were no Drings of Grindleholme Ford.' When the Drings came first, or from whence, none of them knew. Before the Domesday Book was compiled they were there, tilling the land, grinding their own and their neighbours' corn in the windmill that tops Grindleholme Moor, heaping together money and keeping it. Their records show on the pages of local history again and again, and more than once they wrote their names in red letters in the books that deal with national things. They were hard-headed, selfish, domineering men of force and action, and but for a certain conservative spirit which ran through them like the grain through an oak, they had been great lords in the land. As it was, they were great yeomen, and were proud of it. Lords can be made at any time, and princes likewise, but a yeoman must grow on the soil, and with the soil's produce. Through the long war which peers and landowners fought with the yeomen of England, whose land they coveted, the Drings of Grindleholme Ford held their own. In the end they saw the broad yeomanries change into farms, great and small, and men paying tribute to other men for leave to till the soil. They laughed deep down in their hearts at that, for Grindleholme Ford was still theirs, and a thousand acres of land around it.

Hartas Dring, who followed his father in 1821 as head of all the Drings of Grindleholme Ford, made up his mind as he saw them place his father's coffin in its grave that he would not do as his ancestors had done for the past two hundred years. They had been content to keep their own, and to do the best that could be done with it. For two hundred years the Drings had commanded a thousand acres, and in all that time they had not added to their estate by a rood. Hartas swore to himself that where he found a thousand he would leave two thousand. Upon him there had come a desire for greatness such as his forefathers never possessed. He stood in the churchyard while the parson read out of his book, and he looked round him at the fair corn-lands and rolling meadows, and he lusted for them in his heart. 'Man that is born of a woman,' read the parson, 'hath but a short time to live.' 'Pish!' said Hartas Dring to himself. 'Time enow, I warrant, to do all that lies in my heart.' And he hardened himself then and there, and resolved in God's acre and house, and in the presence of his dead father's corpse, to spare neither himself nor his wealth, and to consider neither man nor woman, until he was lord of all the land 'twixt Grindleholme Ford and the sea.

Hartas Dring was then twenty-and-five years old. For the next five-and-twenty years he strove and toiled and plotted and schemed. He cared for neither eating nor drinking. He was up early and at work till late. As for the delights of life, he scorned them. He never looked at a woman unless he was conducting a bargain with one, and he kept no company under his own roof, and sought none in the houses of his neighbours, nor in the inn on market-days. And bit by bit he worked out his own ends. There was a piece of land to sell here, and another there, and they came to him as the needle goes to the magnet. His thousand acres was already three thousand, and when he walked across the churchyard and saw the tombs of his ancestors and remembered his forefathers' motto—'Hold Fast, Dring, And want not Anythinge'—he spat upon the ground in fine scorn, and let his eyes roll across the great stretches of land over which he was lord and master.

II

It came into Hartas Dring's mind as he sat one December night by his fireside that he was now fifty years of age, and must make haste to do two things. Between him and the sea there was but one poor hundred acres of land over which he might not ride his horse. That was the holding of Thurstan Sleightholm. There had been Sleightholms there as long as there had been Drings at Grindleholme, but the Sleightholms were not as the Drings. They had neither increased their store nor held what they had, and now there was but this patch of meadow-land left to Thurstan, the last of them. 'That must be mine,' said Hartas Dring, and he set to work for the thousandth time to devise some means of cozening Thurstan out of the acres to which he clung like a horse-leech. And when he had thought of that, he thought of the other matter which required haste. He must marry—there must be a son to whom all his broad acres could be handed down. So he went to bed swearing a great oath that before next December came round he would marry a wife, and harry Thurstan Sleightholm out of his house and land.

And both these things Hartas Dring did. In June he went to the church, and was married to a girl whose parents gave her to him, not out of her love for him, for she had none, but rather because they owed him more money than they could ever pay. It seemed to Hartas a fair arrangement. He wanted a wife that could bear him a son, and he was willing to buy her. With him life was a question of buying and selling, of values and equivalents. His face was hard as ever as he took his wife home, and when she wept he cursed her as if she had been a dog that whimpers without reason.

As for Thurstan Sleightholm and his land, both fell into Hartas Dring's power as easily as the ripe pear drops into the schoolboy's fingers when he bends the stalk upwards. There was no man in all the East Riding poorer than Thurstan, and in days gone by he had mortgaged his acres for money. What easier than for Hartas Dring to buy up the mortgages, and to fasten his teeth into Thurstan Sleightholm's heart? So it came about that one October morning, when the mists still hung over the land, and a great bank of fog half shut out the wild North Sea from their sight, they came to the beginning of the last act of the tragedy of Thurstan's life.

For Thurstan had fought for house and home, and Hartas Dring had found it necessary to invoke the aid of the law. With the officers and emissaries of the law he now came, and they hunted Thurstan Sleightholm and his wife and children out of the house as hunters dig a fox out of his hole, and when they were out Hartas Dring razed the old farmstead to the ground, so that there was not one stone left higher than another.

When that was over, Thurstan Sleightholm had no more heart in him. He walked down the sandhills to the sea, and where the tide comes swelling in between two high walls of rock he let himself drop into the green water. And so he died, and the tide cast up his body with its eyes wide open, and staring at the sky as if they called upon God for vengeance. Then the fisher-folk who found it shuddered and said that Heaven would surely repay Hartas Dring for forcing a man to this pass; but, since Hartas was their landlord, they held their peace, save to themselves.

But not so did Thurstan's wife. All day and all night she had watched by the beach, for something told her that death was heavy upon her and hers, and she remained there till the body was given back to her by the sea that had slain it. And she looked and said nothing; but, after a time, she turned away and climbed the sandhills, and went across the level land above, the fire of madness in her sunken eyes; and she paused not—save to stand for one moment by the blackened ruins of the house that had once been the dead man's home, and to which he had brought her as his bride, to bear him children, and to comfort him in his loneliness,—until she came to Grindleholme Ford and found Hartas Dring.

Hartas Dring sat at meat in his kitchen. It was his custom to assemble all his family and servants at meal-times. He sat frowning on all, and none dared speak in his presence. But Thurstan Sleightholm's widow spoke. She stood in the doorway, a gaunt figure against the pale October noon-light, and she stretched out her hand that was thin from starvation towards Hartas Dring, and fixed her eye upon him, and she solemnly cursed him in the name of God, and of the Blessed Virgin Mary, and of the White Christ whom his forefathers chose instead of Odin and Thor, and of all saints and martyrs, and she prophesied that never should child of his reign in his stead, but that doom and sorrow should follow him for all the rest of his life.

There was neither man nor woman in the kitchen that did not shudder and feel the blood turn to water in their hearts while the widow spoke,—save one, and he was Hartas Dring.

And he heard her to the end, and when she had finished he rose and took down his great dog-whip and struck her across the face with it, so that she fell shrieking, and after that he bade his men kick her from his doors for a mad woman, and so he sat down again to his meat.

III

Hartas Dring at last was satisfied. For five years he had been lord of all the land 'twixt Grindleholme Ford and the North Sea. That, however, had only satisfied him in part. All that five years he had been filled with a fierce disappointment. His wife had given him no son. He had cursed her for that many a time. Had he married her for aught else than that she should bear him children? Curses upon her that other women should bear children to their husbands and not she! And she had prayed him more than once to kill her, so that he might marry another woman; and Hartas Dring would gladly have answered her prayer but for fear of his own neck, for he hated her because of her barrenness.

And now, at the end of the fifth year, his wife was about to give him a child. When there became a certainty of this the man's heart underwent some change. He was kind in his way to his wife, and careful that naught should interfere with her health. As the time drew near, he made great preparations. There were to be feasting and rejoicing all over the country-side—the highest and the lowest were to celebrate the birth of Hartas Dring's son and heir. He had no doubt as to the child's sex—he had had his way always in all things, and it seemed to him that neither God nor nature could defy or thwart him in this.

And at last the child was born, and it was a boy. Then Hartas Dring was more than satisfied. He kept open house for days, and bade his friends and acquaintances eat and drink to the full. There was no work done thereabouts all that time, and half the men lay drunk about the halls and kitchens because of their zeal in drinking the young heir's health. As for Hartas, he sat at the head of his table night after night, carousing with his cronies, and boasting of the power that his boy should exercise in those parts. And it was while he thus boasted one night that a woman rushed into the great kitchen crying that the child was stolen!

Then there arose the greatest commotion that had ever been known at Grindleholme Ford. Some ran here and some ran there, and for a while Hartas Dring was as a madman. But his hard head at last prevailed over his passion, and he began to ask questions and make inquiries, and then it came out that a half-witted lad had seen Thurstan Sleightholm's widow run swiftly from the house through the byre, and across the grey meadows towards the sea, carrying in her arms something that moved.

When Hartas Dring heard that, he reeled like an oak that receives the last stroke of the woodman's axe, and he said no word to man or woman, but went out and saddled his horse, and rode for the seashore like a madman. And he passed the ruins of Thurstan's house and fancied he heard ghostly cries in the moonlight, but still he rode on, for his heart told him that the woman would make for the spot where her husband died. So it came about that at midnight he rode in the light of a full moon down the steep track between the sand-hills, and came to the spot where Thurstan had died, and there he paused and listened, and heard naught but the lapping of the waves against the black rocks on which he stood. And in that moment Hartas Dring felt his heart turn to flesh for the first time in all his life, and he prayed to God. And as he prayed he heard a weird cry on the cliff above him, and he looked up and saw Thurstan Sleightholm's widow, a spectral figure against the sky, and she held out his child at arm's length and cried to him again.

'Woe to thee, Hartas Dring! Woe and vengeance!' she cried. 'The fulfilling of the curse is at hand—no son of thine shall inherit thy ill-gotten riches!'

And with that she flung the child into the sea beneath, where the tide boiled and foamed amongst the rocks. Then with a great cry Hartas Dring leaped after it, and the sea took him, even as it had taken Thurstan, and so the life went out of him.

In the morning they found the father and the son, the man clutching the child's body, side by side on the beach; and beside them, crooning low music as if she would hush them to sleep, cowered Thurstan Sleightholm's widow with white face, and eyes that burned like live coals in black and cavernous depths.

THE GOLD BODKIN

It's been a weary time that I've laid here waiting to die, and the doctor's been surprised when he's come of a morning to find me still alive. According to him I ought to ha' been dead long since. Folks come in sometimes when I'm lonely and make jest of it, saying that a creaking gate hangs long, and that it's weary waiting for dead men's shoes. As to being likened to a creaking gate I say nought, and as for all they'll get that stand in my shoes, why, it'll be no more than 'll help them to put me in the earth decently. There's twenty gold pounds sewed in the mattress under my bed—you'll mind that, and that it's to bury me with, and to buy me a decent shroud and coffin,—and that's all that I have in this world beside the bits o' sticks in the cottage. There's nobody to benefit, you see, by my death, and so nobody'll give me a thought when I'm gone. It'll be just another old woman out of the world, and nobody will think aught of it—death's common enough, I warrant you!

Ay; he wonders, does the doctor, why I don't die. There was him and the parson's wife in here yesterday, and they were talking about me, because they thought I was asleep. But I wasn't asleep, for all that I had my eyes closed, and I heard every word they said. 'It's queer,' says doctor. 'I can't think how it is that she holds out so long—I expected her dying a month ago.' Then the parson's wife said something about the fine constitution I'd always had, and she was right there, for I've been as strong a woman as ever lived. But it's not the constitution that's kept me alive. It's all gone long since, is that. Look at my arm—all skin and bone, isn't it? No—there's only one person in the world that knows what it is that keeps me from passing, and that's myself. And I'm sick and weary of living any longer, and so I'll tell my story—to you—and after that I shall die just as a candle goes out.

There was parson himself here a day or two ago, and he prayed out of his book and wanted me to confess to him. If I'd been a Papist I would ha' confessed, and felt better for it. But I'm neither Papist nor believer—I never did believe in either God or man after it occurred that I'm going to tell you about—all those ideas were driven out of heart and head at that time. I believe in the devil and in hell, oh yes, because I've proved 'em both,—but in neither man nor God. Man's false and treacherous, and God doesn't interfere, so what was there to make me believe in them? So I've no sins to confess to parson, nor to any one else. It's not a sin that I'm going to tell you about. It doesn't make me uneasy either. I only did what I had to do, and I've never regretted it. But I've kept it locked up in my heart all this time—five-and-fifty years come next June—and I meant to keep it secret till the end. Nobody'll be the better for knowing it—but I shan't pass until it's told, and I want to pass. It's weary work lying here waiting for death.

You mightn't think it, but sixty years ago I was the handsomest maiden in all the Riding—everybody, man and woman alike, said so. I was tall and strong, and my face and figure, as old Squire Stubbs used to say, was like a queen's. I 've stood in front of a bit o' looking-glass and admired myself for an hour at a time, and I 've said to myself when I was occupied in that way that there wasn't a wench in the country that had such glossy black hair or such bright eyes or such colour in lips and cheek as I had. And at that time I was main proud o' my beauty, never thinking, poor fool that I was, that beauty 's one o' the devil's baits. Small reason did I have to be proud or thankful for mine. If I 'd been born as ugly as Red-headed Poll, that everybody made fun of, it would ha' been better for me.

Of course, I 'd lovers—plenty of 'em, and at one time I could ha' taken pick and choice of half a dozen good men. But there never was but one man that I cared more than a crooked ha'penny for, and that was Geoffrey Heathcott, of the Mote Farm. He was a better sort of man, for his land was his own, and he had the right to call himself a gentleman, though he did farm his own acres. You 'll recollect nought o' the Mote Farm—it 's no more than a ruin now, and the land 's sold long since to Squire Clifford; but in those days it was a bonny place ; there was ivy and clematis on the old grey walls, and the garden was beautiful with trees and shrubs and flowers. We had many a happy day there, and remembered them after with curses.

I went to the Mote Farm as dairymaid just before old Mrs. Heathcott died. Geoffrey Heathcott was a young man then, and folks said he 'd marry and settle down now that his mother was dead. But they were wrong there, for he made no sign o' marrying. He was curious in his way—a good farmer, but given to reading books and wandering about the garden o' nights as if he was poetry-making. He never associated with the folks hereabouts, and they called him proud and queer because of it. But why should he ha' made himself cheap to them, seeing that he was cleverer than any of 'em? I always liked him the better because he kept himself high above all of 'em.

It was a lonely place, the Mote Farm, and I was a good deal alone in the dairy, and Geoffrey Heathcott used to come in there and talk to me. And bit by bit we got fond of each other, and there were meetings in the garden and in the fields, and at last we were lovers—though he was master and I was maid. If there 's a God, as parson says there is, that knows everything, He only knows how I loved that man—ay, and what I gave up for him. For at last I was everything to Geoffrey Heathcott that a woman can be to a man—but he never made me his wife.

There was no one ever knew of it. It was so easy in a quiet place like that to keep everything secret; and beside, who 'd ever ha' suspected that a man like him should ha' fallen in love with a girl like me—whose father was shepherd to a working farmer? So it went on for a year or more, and I was content enough, for he 'd spoken as fair words as ever man could to a woman. There was some reason why he couldn't marry, he said, until a certain time had gone by, but as soon as it had gone by he would marry me at church, and all would be right. And, of course, I trusted him—what woman wouldn't? I was ready to believe everything that Geoffrey Heathcott told me, just because I loved him.

It was one night in spring that he came to me, and told me he was obliged to leave home for a week or two—he'd business in London that required his presence there. I made no objection, of course, though I bear in mind well enough that I wished I could ha' gone with him. I remember a deal of what we had to say to each other that night. I never doubted him for a minute. He was going next day, and that night he gave me a present—a gold bodkin that had been given to one of his ancestors by some great body in gone-by times. It 's sewed up with my twenty gold pounds in the mattress, and you 'll see that it 's put in my coffin after I 'm dead. It 's a fine bit of gold—strong and straight and sharp at the end as a needle, and maybe somebody that has to do wi' my body when I 'm dead might take a fancy to it for its value, but it 's mine, and I 'll have it in the coffin wi' me—you must pin it on to the shroud, just above my heart.

Geoffrey Heathcott had been gone maybe a week when there came to the Mote Farm one o' them lawyer bodies—a cold, stony-faced man that looked right through you. He brought another lawyer with him—Lawyer Applegarth, of Cornchester—and they were with Tobias Garforth, the hind, in the little parlour for the best of an hour. And at the end o' that time they called all of us in—there were six servants, men and women, in the house—and told us their news. Geoffrey Heathcott had gone to Australia, and wasn't coming back for years, and Tobias was to farm the land at easy terms for himself, and to pay rent to the lawyers, and, as for the rest of us, we were paid our wages and something over there and then, and we could re-engage with Tobias or not as we pleased. And that was all.

I had to stand there, you 'll understand, and hear it like all the rest of 'em without making a sign. But it seemed to me that something turned my heart to stone in that moment, and I went out and set to on my work in the dairy as if I were a machine instead of a live woman. It was a goodish bit before I could fairly think things over, but at last it struck me that Geoffrey Heathcott couldn't have really gone —he would write to me from London in a day or two and send me money to go to him, and he would take me with him to Australia. So I was cheerful again, and hoped for the best. And after that the days went by until a week's end came, and still I had no word of him ; and a month passed, and at last I knew that Geoffrey Heathcott had forsaken me.

I 've heard folk say that love turns to hate, but I don't know whether it 's true, for I loved him as fierce as ever, only I hated him too. If I could ha' found him then I 'd ha' killed him—but I 'd ha' kissed his dead lips as fondly as ever. Nothing but killing him would have satisfied me, though I loved him as I 'd always done.

It was four years after that when they began to talk in the village about Geoffrey Heathcott's coming home. It was Tobias Garforth that set it about. He said that Geoffrey Heathcott had made a deal of money in Australia, and was coming back to live at the Mote Farm. Only it wasn't to be a farm any longer, but a grand gentleman's house. Some believed Tobias's news and some didn't; but it was true, and presently the lawyers came and gave out a lot of instructions, and there were all sorts of alterations made at the Mote Farm, and the builders and paper-hangers came, and there were great loads of furniture sent down from London town, and folks that went to peep in at the window said it was like a palace, and much finer than Squire Clifford's place at the Park.

But I never went near, for I 'd heard a matter talked of that made the blood in my veins hotter than fire. They said that Geoffrey Heathcott was going to be married to some rich man's daughter in London, and that he and his wife were coming straight home to the Mote Farm. His wife?—as if I wasn't his wife as much as any woman could be! When I heard that and knew that it was true, I went out one night and swore to God that I 'd have vengeance on Geoffrey Heathcott if I suffered for it.

It was a summer's evening when Geoffrey Heathcott and the girl he 'd married came home. I never knew whether they 'd been married that day or a day or two before, but she was in her bridal finery, and he sat by her in the carriage looking as proud of her as could be. There was a great to-do in the village—they 'd put up an archway of green stuff between the King's Arms and Farmer Topps's house, and they took out the horses and dragged the carriage up the street, and there were crowds everywhere. But nobody saw me, for I peeped through the cottage window at them and cursed Geoffrey Heathcott in my heart—and yet I loved him all the time. As soon as I set eyes on him I knew that I loved him more than ever, and yet I swore to be revenged on him. For he'd hurt me past endurance, and it was only fair, wasn't it, that he should be made to suffer for it?

I don't know what it was that made me take the gold bodkin in my hand when I went out that night, nor why I was holding it so firmly when I crept through the garden of the Mote Farm, and peeped in at the windows. There was a light in every room, it seemed to me, and all the things were very grand; but I saw nought but Geoffrey Heathcott and the woman whom he'd put in my place. And I saw what turned everything to blood—the caresses that he gave her that should have been mine; and when I saw it, I knew what there was for me to do.

It was so easy to hide myself in that house—I'd done it a hundred times for love's sake. It was easy, too, to get into their chamber; but it seemed to me that all I did was done in a dream. For at last, in the quietest part of the night, I stood by their bed and looked at them. There was a faint moonlight in the room, and I saw the woman's face, but Geoffrey Heathcott's face was in shadow. And at last—it seemed a long time, somehow—I felt for her heart, where it beat beneath the white linen, and I drove the gold bodkin into it and held it there. And there was scarce a movement, and what there was didn't wake the sleeping man, for Geoffrey Heathcott was always a sound sleeper. But the woman was dead, and her blood was on the point of the bodkin, and when I looked at her in the moonlight there was just a speck of blood on the white of her breast. And then I stole away and left Geoffrey Heathcott alive, so that he might be tortured before his time came.

But in the morning Geoffrey Heathcott was dead too. For he woke and found his young wife dead at his side, and his grief was too great for him, and he shot himself with his pistol before ever he gave alarm of her death. And then the weight that had been so long on my head seemed to lift, and my heart was lighter.

It's to be pinned on to my shroud. I'll come back and haunt you if that isn't done. With the twenty gold pounds it is, in the mattress—it's strong and sharp as ever. I can remember the feel of it—how it went into her heart so straight and true.

THE VOW

BARBARA KENT came out of her little cottage and stood at the gate looking up and down the road. It was very early morning; the sun still made a rosy curtain of the eastern horizon, and the gossamer webs hung thick and white on the hedgerows. There was no one in the village street or on the chapel hill. The blinds were drawn in the chapel windows and in the windows of the farmhouse over the way. Nobody seemed stirring but herself. She waited a moment longer at the gate, and looked about her with a vague curiosity in her face. She had seen the same things every morning for years, but it seemed to her that they now possessed a new significance. She glanced at them again—at the chapel and the farmhouse and at the orchard and at the red-roofed cottages, and then she went into her cottage again and sat down and folded her hands in her lap and waited. And as she waited she prayed. 'Pray God!' she said, 'that they come soon and take me away before the neighbours are astir, lest all the village see my shame!' This was what she prayed, having still some of the old Kent pride left in her.

Barbara Kent was five-and-sixty years of age. Every one in Queen's Malbis knew her slight figure and pale, refined face. Dressed in rusty black, always threadbare, always neat, she had been a conspicuous figure at the Methodist chapel for more years than all but the elderly people could remember. When she first went there to worship she sat with the other Kents in a pew for which sitting-money had to be paid. Of late years she had found a place in the free seats amongst the old men and women and the farmers' lads. She sat there with an ancient dignity and well-preserved seriousness that at once distinguished her from her surroundings. It was easy to see that she had come down in the world.

A mile away from Queen's Malbis there stands a solitary homestead, set in a ring of beech and elm trees. You can see its high gables, the red-tiled barns, the grey tower of its ancient pigeon-cote, for many a mile as you go about the land in that corner of the wapentake. It is a lonely place, but the house is built of solid stone, damp-proof and wind-proof, and in the great orchard at its side there are fruit-trees the yield of which is noted throughout the whole Riding. The name of this solitary homestead is Ravenscroft, and the church books show that there were Kents of Ravenscroft from the time of William and Mary onward. They were tenant-farmers, and bore the reputation of doing their duty to the land better than most of their sort. That, of course, was natural, seeing that as soon as one Kent died his eldest son stepped into his place. It came to be a recognised thing that there should be a Kent of Ravenscroft, and therefore every Kent did his best with the land, so that his son and his son's son should get good out of it.

Matthias Kent married and had one child by his wife—the girl Barbara. When his wife died he remained single for some time, but at last he married again, and his wife gave him a son, which was what he most desired. He gave this boy the name of Robert, and ever after its birth he chiefly occupied himself in watching or amusing it. He carried the boy with him wherever he went, sometimes wrapped in a shawl on his saddle-bow, sometimes huddled up in old coats and rugs on the seat of his tax-cart. When the lad was seven he made the tailor clothe him after the fashion of a man, and the next Saturday he took him to Sicaster market, and had him in to the ordinary. Some of the farmers laughed at Matthias for this proceeding, and patted the boy on the head; but others frowned, and said that if the lad was brought up in that way he would come to no good. But these said little to Matthias, for it was plain to see that his heart was wrapped up in his son, and that he would take counsel with nobody as to the right way of bringing him up.

Matthias's second wife died when Robert was twelve years old, and within a year of her decease Matthias himself lay sick unto death on the great four-poster with the blue hangings. He went out one morning hale and hearty, and came back dying ere noon had struck. Because he was a man from whom it was neither wise nor possible to conceal aught, they told him that he must soon die, and advised him, if he had affairs to arrange, to lose no time in setting about their disposal. When he had heard this, Matthias turned all of them out of his room and bade them send Barbara to his bedside. Barbara came, keeping back her tears, because she knew that her father hated to see women weep. She was then a girl of nineteen years, sweet and fair, with the most pleasant expression of human goodness in her face. She knelt at the bedside and took her father's hand within her own.

'Barbara,' said Matthias, 'I am dying;—in one hour—only one short hour!—from now I shall be as dead as all the folk in Malbis churchyard. 'Tis a hard thing—I had reckoned to live at least twenty years longer. But that's no use—the time is short. Girl, listen to me. All is settled—Lawyer Flood has all the papers. Until Robbie is twenty-one years of age the farm will be managed by Lawyer Flood and you, and a hind that you and Flood will engage. When Robbie comes to his manhood, it will be his—the Squire has given me his promise for all this, Barbara—

and so will the money I have made, and what they made who came before me. It has always been so with us Kents of Ravenscroft. You understand me?'

Barbara understood him, and said so, stroking his hand the while. He rolled his head towards her, and went on speaking.

'Now, Barbara, there is one thing that you must do. It is you that must look after Robbie while ever there is need of it. Swear to me neither to marry nor to depart from him so long as the lad has need of your help. Swear it on the Scriptures, and let me die easy.'

There was no thought in Barbara's mind at that moment of what the consequences of this vow might be. Her one idea was to gratify the last wish of her father. She rose up and fetched the great Bible, and laying her hand on its open pages she swore never to leave her brother, either for marriage or for any other reason, so long as he had need of her.

After that Matthias bade her go away and fetch Robert. When the brother and sister went back to the chamber their father was dead, and Barbara's great responsibility had its beginning.

Until Robbie was twenty-one everything

seemed to go well with the Kents of Ravenscroft. Lawyer Flood and Barbara hired a good hind, and, Barbara herself being a clever manager, there was much money earned and saved and put away against the time when Robbie came of age. Then everything was to be his, except a thousand pounds devised to Barbara. It seemed a poor amount, for Matthias had left a good deal of money; but Lawyer Flood said that from time immemorial a thousand pounds had been the portion of the Kent womankind, and Barbara was satisfied. She was one of those rare creatures who never think of self; her sole aim in life was to discharge her duty to Robbie. Always deeply religious, she regarded her vow as a most sacred obligation. She watched over her brother jealously. No mother could have been more anxious for his prosperity and welfare. She interested herself in all that he did; in his boyish pleasures; his schooling; his notions and ideas; she coaxed him to confide and believe in her. The lad gave her no anxiety during his boyish days—he took life lightly, it was true, and was fonder of his pleasures than of the serious things in which Barbara took delight, but beyond that he seemed to be free from vice and disposed to live a clean and sober life.

It was when Barbara was twenty-six and her brother nineteen years of age that Michael Burton fell in love with her. He was a farmer in Queen's Malbis, sober, steady, well-to-do—the very man to make her a good husband. She let him court her for a year before she would consent to give him a definite answer to the question that he had put to her more than once. Then she promised to marry him, but, remembering her vow (which, indeed, was always present to her mind), she stipulated that he should not claim her until it was abundantly apparent that Robbie had no further need. Burton accepted the stipulation joyfully; it seemed to him that as Robbie was twenty-one he would settle down to manage Ravenscroft by himself, and that Barbara would then be free. So he and Barbara were duly betrothed, and there was a new light in her life.

It was about six months previous to Robbie's coming of age that Barbara first had any anxiety about him. He went with companions to Sicaster Fair, and came home intoxicated.

Barbara spoke to him gravely and gently, begging him never to offend again in like manner. Robbie laughed and promised. He had some plausible excuse for his transgression, and Barbara believed him, and, after she had scolded him, made up for the scolding by added kindness. But in a month Robbie was drunk again. This time Barbara went on her knees to him and begged him to bethink himself of the consequences which must ensue if he persisted in a life of dissipation. Robbie laughed at her again, and finally flew into a temper at her continued pleading.

'A fine thing!' said he, stalking with lifted head from the parlour. 'A fine thing, indeed, that a man may not take his liquor without so much caterwauling and mewling from a parcel of women! Stick to your hymns and your cat-lap, sister, and leave me alone. I have been cooped up here too long, and am now minded to see something of the world.'

Then Barbara knew that she must make good the promise she had given to her father. And she stood there looking down the long vista of years to come, and she asked herself questions that she could not answer.

As soon as Robbie Kent attained his twenty-first year everything came into his hands. He was tenant, and therefore master, of Ravenscroft, and owner of all the money that generations of Kents had hoarded together. Now, during the previous half-year he had made many companions, none of them of the sort likely to help him to lead a good life, but rather inclined to assist him in spending his substance in riotous living. Barbara soon found that everything was to be changed. Robbie came home drunk on market nights, and to her expostulations and entreaties he replied first with ribald laughter and then with curses. He began bringing his pothouse companions to the homestead, where they kept up unholy revels through half the night, while Barbara wept and prayed in her own room. And so things progressed, going from bad to worse.

There would have been small hope for Robbie at this period, so far as his career as a farmer was concerned, if it had not been for his sister. The Squire, loth to turn a Kent off the land which their family had farmed for generations, was still bound to take notice of

Robbie's foolish ways. Barbara pleaded and persuaded. She did the overseeing herself; she was out early and late; she tramped across the fields or rode to market while her brother idled his time or wasted his money at one or other of the neighbouring towns. Thus she kept things going, and the Squire had his rent to the day. Of that, indeed, he had no fear—there was money enough and to spare. But he and others nodded their heads, and said, wisely enough, that the money would not last for ever.

As for Michael Burton, he was sorely tried. He loved Barbara truly, and grieved to see her wasting the best years of her life over her scapegrace brother. Once he asked her to forswear her vow and leave Robbie to his fate, and come to him and be happy. Barbara listened and replied; and after she had spoken Michael knew that nothing, not even love, would turn her from the fulfilment of the vow she had sworn to Matthias as he lay on his deathbed.

When this state of things had lasted some four years, during the whole of which time Barbara vainly endeavoured to persuade her brother to give up his wild habits and settle down, there came a gleam of hope to both Barbara and Michael Burton. Robbie fell in love. The girl was young, modest, and good, and it became plain that she had some influence over him. Barbara went to her, and begged her to use her influence, and after that Robbie remained sober and conducted himself soberly for some time. But his sweetheart was delicate and fragile, and in the spring which should have witnessed their marriage she died of consumption. For a while Robbie's grief kept him still sober, but ere long he fell in with his old companions, and they tempted him, and he gave way to his old evil courses, and his behaviour was worse than before.

And now Michael Burton came to Barbara with set face and determined eyes, and bade her take him into the parlour so that he might speak to her privately. 'Barbara,' said he, 'this sort of thing cannot go on. Robbie is bound to go his own way. You cannot turn him from his evil. He will return to it again and again — nothing will change him. My dear, it is not right that you should waste your life upon him. I love you, and I have waited a long time. Now, Barbara, I can wait no longer. You must choose between him and me.'

'I cannot,' she said. 'I cannot, Michael. I have not the power. I promised my father.'

'Barbara,' he said, 'think a moment. If you marry me you can still look after your brother. I will help you. Why——'

'It is no good, Michael,' she answered; 'I swore neither to marry any man nor to leave Robbie while Robbie had need of me. And his need is great.'

'Then we must say good-bye to each other,' said Michael Burton. 'I have loved you long and true, Barbara, but I cannot let things go on in this way. Is it impossible for you to marry me?'

'It is,' she said. 'I cannot leave Robbie. I will stay with him till one of us is taken. Perhaps I may save him yet.'

'You will never save him,' answered Michael bitterly. 'And you will wreck your own life into the bargain.'

Then they clasped hands, and he made as if to draw her to him and kiss her lips, but she motioned him away, and said, 'God bless and keep you, Michael!' and so left him. And when he had gone from the house she went to her chamber and knelt down and prayed long, beseeching God for mercy with much weeping, and at last came downstairs, comforted, with a great peace shining in her eyes.

But the mercy for which Barbara prayed came not—at least, on this earth. For her brother sank deeper and deeper into the mire in which he loved to wallow, and nothing but disgrace and shame followed his steps. And at last he was turned off his farm, and he and Barbara left the house in which there had been Kents for six generations. It was little use attempting it, even after this, but Barbara still tried to save him. She persuaded him to take a smaller farm in the neighbourhood, and thither they went, she beseeching him to mend his ways and retrieve his character. For a while he tried to do well, but ere long the old habits asserted themselves, and so he went from bad to worse. Barbara strove and strove, and worked hard, rising early and going to bed late, to keep her brother's head above water, but it was no use ; he flung his money away as if it had been dirt, never heeding the sacrifices she had made for him with such patient fidelity.

And at last, in spite of all that she could do, the end came, and Robbie found himself sold up, the last penny of his wealth gone, and himself a pauper.

Barbara was then a toil-worn woman of fifty. Care had hardened her face, and sorrow had whitened her hair, but she was still faithful to her vow. Robbie was now left without one penny to rattle against another, but she had her thousand pounds still untouched, together with the accumulated interest. She went to live in the cottage by the chapel at Queen's Malbis, and made a home for Robbie under its roof. She tried to steady him, and hoped to succeed now that it was not possible for him to have so much money to spend.

But Robbie, knowing of his sister's little fortune, was not minded to go without the means of satisfying his wickedness, and he took counsel with certain of his friends as to how he might possess himself of it. And thus it came about that one day there came news to Barbara that her brother had forged her name, and had drawn her money from the place where she had lodged it, and had fled.

She was now penniless. Whether or not she

at that time looked back with regret on her wasted life it is impossible to say, for she made no sign. It may have been that she wished for the time to come over again so that she might have taken Michael Burton's advice to break her vow and marry him. He had long since left the neighbourhood, and had married and done well, and had perhaps forgotten her. But she had not forgotten. She forgot nothing —not even Robbie. She set to work to earn her own living. She sewed, she went to help in the farmhouses, she was glad to do anything that she was fit and had strength for. Day by day she toiled, having a horror of the bread of charity. On Sunday she sat in the free seats at the chapel, a rusty black figure whose very poverty commanded respect. And Sunday or week-day she prayed unceasingly for the wanderer's return. For she dreaded to meet her father in the world of shadows and find herself unable to give him a good account of his son.

And Robbie came back. Where he had been and how he had spent his time no one knew, for he had no chance to tell them. He was found lying dead one morning by the roadside at the entrance to the village. His clothes were ragged and dirty, there was no money in his pockets, and his face was the face of an old man.

Barbara had saved money for her own burial. She took it from its hiding-place and used it to bury her brother in the vault underneath the church, where Matthias and many another Kent already lay asleep. That done, she went back to her daily toil. People said that she looked more satisfied. They thought she must be relieved to know that Robbie was at last powerless to vex and distress her. But of all these things she said nothing to any one. She went on her way silently and without complaint, until at last sickness overtook her, and she found herself without means of support. She tided over the sickness, but the poverty stuck, and at last there was nothing left for her but the shelter of the workhouse. It was hard, and she felt it to be hard, that the last of the Kents should come to that, and so when the day came for her removal to the house she begged the man who was to drive her there to come with his cart before the neighbours were up, so that no one might see her go.

All these things she thought of, letting her mind wander over the past as she waited in her little cottage. How different it all might have been! She had known nothing but sadness and grief, weeping and sore trouble, all her life. She might have had love and quiet joy, the affection of a good man, the caresses of little children, the assurance of comfortable old age, the thousand-and-one delights that spring——

A sound woke her out of her reverie. She looked up and saw, waiting outside her cottage door, the conveyance that was to carry her away to the workhouse.

ERE THE SUN WENT DOWN

I

'WHO cares?' said Cicely. She snatched up her grain-measure from the kitchen table, and went out into the sunlight, letting the heavy door fall to behind her with a clash that shook the thick walls. In her hazel eyes there was temper, and round about the dainty curves of mouth and chin an expressive evidence of naughtiness. She gave John a quick glance over her shoulder ere she vanished, and John saw these things, and was troubled, in spite of the spasm of laughter that shot through him. Because of laughter and trouble, and of the great love that welled up in his heart for froward Cicely, he rose from his chair by the fireside, and went slowly across the floor and opened the door and looked out.

Cicely stood in the yard—a sweet and glowing picture of vigorous young womanhood in the fresh morning sunlight. Her gown was lilac-hued, and the slight breeze that came from beyond the apple-trees wrapped it closely about her ripe figure. On her cheeks there burnt a glow of vexation ; but it seemed to John that no peach, warmed and kissed by the sun against his garden wall, had ever shown such perfect colour, inviting almost to madness, as that. Nor was there ever a rose-leaf, crumpled by the weight of a bee, that could pucker itself into such a delicious attraction as the full, red lips that were now curved into a bewitching naughtiness. He looked and looked, a slight smile of indulgent affection playing about his mouth, and then he burst into laughter.

John's laughter, strident and hearty rather than musical and refined, grated on Cicely's ears. She gave him a quick glance, lightning-like in its passage from the hazel eyes to the grey ones, and then she turned her back upon him with a little toss of the head, which made John think of the play-actors whom he had once seen in Sicaster market-place on statutes day. There were fowls and ducks and a stray goose that had escaped its fellows at Cicely's feet, and to them she threw handful after handful of corn. And because John was there, and wanting to talk to her, she began to talk to the fowls, and, finally, to sing at the top of her voice.

John turned away at last, still laughing. He went into the house, and remained there several minutes, but when he came out again Cicely was still busied with her fowls. She gave him a quick glance, and noticed the whip that he carried in his right hand. When she saw that, Cicely's temper turned to wickedness.

'So you are going?' she asked. 'You are?'

'I mun go, lass,' answered John. 'I ha' no choice i' t' matter.'

'And you're going without me?' she said.

'There's no choice i' that either, lass,' said John. 'One on us must stop at home to-day, and since I can't, thou mun. Come, lass, come, what odds is missing one Sicaster Fair? Gow, I wish I wor goin' to stop at home i'steead o' goin' yonder!'

'You!' she said, her temper hot and careless, 'you! Ah, you're a nice 'un to go to a fair! You'll sit in a bar-parlour and smoke and drink and take no heed of a bit of merry-makin'.

But I've never missed a Sicaster Fair yet, and it's hard 'at I can't go to this.'

'A 'll come home as soon as ever my business is finished, lass,' said John soothingly. 'And I'll bring thee a new ribbon, or summut pretty —so gi' us a kiss, and let me go.'

Cicely threw up her head. She caught up the grain-measure, and made for the kitchen door.

'Keep your ribbons!' she said. 'What good are ribbons to a woman 'at's no better than a slave? I've no time for ribbons, marry.'

'Come and gi' us a kiss, tell thee!' laughed John. 'Slave?—gow, I think it's me 'at's a slave, my pretty. Come on—let's hev' a touch o' thi lips before I go.'

'Wait till you come back!' said Cicely. She was inside the door by that time, and she slammed it in John's face. She stood with her hand on the sneck, and waited. She half-expected, and more than half-wished, that he would open the door and kiss her, whether she would or no. But presently she heard his heavy footsteps pass away on the flags outside. Then she caught the clatter of the mare's iron shoes on the cobbles, and she ran to the window and looked out between the pots of geranium.

John was riding out of the yard. It seemed to Cicely that his head was bent, as if in disappointment.

II

The afternoon was one of golden light and dreamy sleepiness. The sunlight falling on the old farmstead made rare pictures of the red roof and grey walls, and of the gorgeous sunflowers and dahlias in the garden. Cicely sat under a lilac-tree and sewed. Her temper had not yet passed away, for she was powerless to forget the delights of Sicaster Fair. While she sat there, sewing her own linen, or darning John's thick socks, what magnificence and excitement there was going on in the old market-place! It was cruel that John should prevent her from going. The house might surely have looked after itself for one afternoon—lonely as it was, there were few chances that strangers would come that way and molest it. But then John was so particular about his bits of things—he fumed and worried over every little matter. He might surely have arranged things so that she could go to the fair—but, of course, she was his wife, and therefore a slave, and so it was no good repining. But Cicely did repine in spite of her resolve not to.

A young woman came over the sunlighted fields by a narrow path between the corn, and caught sight of Cicely as she turned into the lane. She advanced to the privet hedge, and looked over, standing on tip-toe. 'Nay!' she said, 'I niver did! Why, what are you doing there, Cicely? I thowt you 'd ha' been off to t' fair long sin'. You 're late.'

'I 'm not goin',' answered Cicely.

'Not goin'! Why, I niver knew you to miss a fair i' your life!'

'But I 'm married now,' said Cicely.

'Eh, dear! Wouldn't John let you go?'

Cicely explained. The face looking over the privet hedge assumed an expression of scorn, pity, and contempt.

'I should tak' no notice, lass,' said its mouth. 'Go and put on your things and come on wi' me. You moän't let John hev' t' upper hand like that theer—it 's t' greatest mistake that a woman can mak'. You mun show him 'at you 're bahn to suit your sen. Come on to t' fair, and if he says owt when you come home, tell him 'at you're his wife, and not his slave. That's t' way to manage men—I know!'

Cicely mused. The advice seemed to accord with her inclination, for she was proud and headstrong, and it hurt her to feel that she was yielding obedience to a man. The adamantine nature of John's refusal to take her with him had made her to chafe and fret—she felt like a young mare that has been under curb and chain until the point of endurance is past, and a bolt becomes inevitable.

'Come in, and sit down for ten minutes,' said Cicely. She led the way into the house, and installed her friend in John's elbow-chair, while she ran upstairs. In a quarter of an hour she came down, a deeper red in her cheeks, and a brighter glow in her eyes. The girl in the chair broke into loud praises of Cicely's gown and of her gold earrings. The fair would look more like itself when Cicely got there.

'I hope John won't see us,' said Cicely as she locked the door. 'He'd be that vexed 'at I hadn't done as he said. But I must see them play-actors again. Come on, let's walk fast.'

They turned into the fields, two blots of colour

against the splendid monotony of the golden crops that half-enveloped them. Far away in the distance the spire of Sicaster Church invited them onward.

III

Cicely came out of the booth, closely attended by Bella. The play was over, the curtain had fallen; already the actors were making ready for the next performance.

'Weren't it lovely!' sighed Bella. 'Eh dear, I fair cried when the handsome young lord and his sweetheart were parted. Eh—and how grand they did talk and walk about!—it were fair beautiful to see how they swung t' tails o' their dresses round 'em.'

'Well, it's over now!' said Cicely. 'All 'at's nice seems to come to a quick end, somehow. Bella, I'm going home now. I must get home before John comes in, and if I go now I shall.'

'Well, you are a silly!' answered Bella. 'Laws!—why, there's all the fun to come on yet. We hevn't seen t' wild beasts, and there's a stone man ower yonder, and the fat woman, and them conjurers, and there's t' panorama in t' Beastfair—we hevn't seen any o' them.'

'You can stop and see 'em,' said Cicely. 'I 've seen t' play-actin', and now I 'll go. Good-bye, Bella—you 'll find somebody to go round with. Good-bye.'

She hurried away through the crowd, unheeding Bella's half-sneering remark as to her foolishness. Cicely was miserable. Something in the tinsel passion of the poor play-actors had stirred up a vein of emotion in her, and she suddenly recognised that she was treating John badly. She wanted to get out of the rickety canvas booth and run home there and then, but she and Bella were tightly packed in the crowd, and escape was impossible. Now that she was free she hurried away from the market-place by quiet courts and alleys until she emerged upon the country road that led homewards. She looked fearfully up and down its white expanse, dreading to see John, not because of his anger, but rather because she felt that she had treated him meanly So much had one poor touch of sentiment mouthed from the lips of a half-starved strolling player, done for her rebellious heart.

'He trusted me,' said Cicely, as she turned into the fields and hurried through the tall corn, 'and it was mean to go and leave t' house as I did. If only he 's not at home when I get there, I 'll make up to him for it—he shall have t' nicest bit o' supper 'at I can manage.'

The sun was hot, but she hurried on, sometimes running between the corn, sometimes resting for a second or two at a stile to fan herself with her handkerchief. It was while she rested thus that she remembered that John had gone away disappointed of the kiss with which she always sent him about his business. The remembrance made her still more uncomfortable. In all their short married life of five months she had never refused him a kiss until that morning. It hurt her at the time, and she would have given worlds to have been able to subdue her pride and call him back. But now when the fading afternoon brought deeper thoughts, and gratified temper had produced a strong harvest of remorse, her crime against love seemed to assume awful dimensions, and she ran on in an agony of self-upbraiding.

At last she reached the old house. The door was still fast, the key hung behind the shutter where she and John placed it if either went out while the other was not at home. She ran upstairs and tore off her finery, and dashed into the yard to see that all was well there. She counted geese and ducks and poultry with the accuracy of a mathematician, and sighed with relief to find that no thief nor tramp had visited them. Then she ran indoors and stirred the fire into a blaze, and set on the kettle. She placed John's slippers by his easy-chair, and laid his old coat ready to his hand when he should come in. Then she busied herself with the table, spreading her whitest cloth on the white deal, bringing out the best her larder could afford. Then the kettle began to sing, and Cicely sang too, and so the kitchen was full of melody as sweet as the flowers in the window-sill.

Cicely suddenly grew silent. What should she say to John? Should she tell him that she had sinned against his wishes, and treated him meanly? Was there need of it? He didn't know she 'd gone, and he hadn't seen her, and perhaps no one would tell him supposing any of their friends had seen her—they 'd think that she had gone there with John. No, surely there was no reason to tell him that she 'd not done as he wished. And yet Cicely felt that she ought to confess and be absolved. It would be so much more comfortable—and John was so ready to forgive. But her pride rose again, and so she sat undecided and wondering——

A sound of cartwheels at the gate, a heavy foot on the gravel, the murmur of voices, a hesitating tap at the door, roused her from her reverie. She ran across to the door and opened it. Before she saw the man's face at the door or the group at the gate she knew that sorrow had come to her. She put out her hand as if to keep the men off, and ran down the gravel path.

'Do thee wait a bit, my dear!' said the old man who had knocked at the door in his office of news-breaker. 'Do thee wait, poor dear, Lord help thee!'

But she ran on. She stopped only when she had pushed her way through the men and thrown aside the sheet from John's dead face.

Even then there was neither cry nor sigh from Cicely's white lips. She looked round her as a child looks round a chamber of mystery. She saw the red roof, the grey gables, the sunflowers nodding against the glossy privet hedge, and suddenly she realised that her problem was solved. It was now too late to confess: too late to be forgiven.

POOR DANIEL

For three-and-fifty years life and the world had been to Daniel the most dismal realities. If he had ever possessed the capacity to understand things, it is scarcely probable that he would have allowed himself to live. Nature, however, had mercifully endowed him with an oxlike power of dumb endurance—he therefore went on his way, suffering and bearing, with little or no regard to his own feelings. To analyse anything was beyond his power—self-consciousness had no place within his mental equipment. All he did was just to live, taking things as they came, and showing no more feeling with respect to them than is shown by the forgotten beast of burden left to starvation and cold in the corner of some desolate close.

It was well for Daniel that Nature had provided him with so large a capacity to suffer, for in other respects she had been more than niggardly to him. One of his legs was some inches shorter than its fellow, and where his right eye should have been there was nothing but a foul scar. Thus his gait resembled the painful movements of a crab, and his face appalled whatever child looked at him. But against these afflictions Daniel set up that steady endurance which characterised him throughout his days, and with its aid he forgot the short leg and the lost eye. It was no virtue, inherent or cultivated, that enabled him to do so, but simply the result of Nature's provision in that respect.

All his life, from early infancy onward, Daniel had known the meaning of the word labour. There were five of them at home in the little cottage near the church at Queen's Malbis—the father, mother, Daniel himself, and two sisters. The father was a weakly man, who carried the signs of death in his face for many a year before Death finally claimed him. Because of his weakness and of the invalid mother in the arm-chair by the fireside, Daniel was put to work as soon as he was high enough to reach a horse's bridle. He rose long before the sun and made the fire in the little cottage-home ere he set out, limping and shivering, for the farmstead. All day he toiled, sometimes in the fold, sometimes in the mistal or stable, sometimes knee-deep in the wet turnips, until night sent him home again, still shivering, and always limping. All this toil produced but little result in the shape of wealth, and yet it had been hard work to keep the wolf from the door without the few shillings which Daniel brought home o' Saturday nights. He was fortunate in one respect—there was never lack of work for him. In the three-and-fifty years during which Daniel lived, there was not one day of all those that came after he first began working on which he did not continue his labour. Some people of his acquaintance kept festival on Christmas Day and Good Friday, and took their week's holiday at Martinmas; others, having worked six days out of seven, did nothing on Sunday save eat, sleep, and idle their time. Daniel, however, kept no festival, and was only slightly less busy on Sundays than on other days of the week. He worked as hard on a public holiday as other men do in harvest, and on Sunday he milked the cows at morning and night, and did odd jobs into the bargain.

In boyhood he was called Lame Daniel; it was not until his father died that he gained the distinguishing title by which he was ever afterwards known. 'Poor' in his case meant unfortunate, unlucky, much put upon. For the father was dead, and the mother was a hopeless invalid of the sort that lives a long, long time; and of the two sisters, Martha was dying by inches, and Susan was bound to look to the home, and would, therefore, do nothing towards earning her own living. Daniel was then twenty years of age—a gaunt, hungry-looking thing, with wild face and unkempt hair, and an eye that seemed as if it were perpetually endeavouring to discover something undiscoverable. When his mother told him that henceforward he would have to provide for all of them, he made no more answer than a nod and a grunt. He had known it all along; indeed, he had never known anything else. There was, therefore, no new departure to make, save to go to the master and ask for a rise in his wages. Because he was a hard worker, and did more than any two men on the farm, he got what he asked for. After that, for thirty-three years, Daniel went on working steadily. The old mother sat in the old chair by the fire, always dying but never dead; Martha lingered ten years ere Daniel buried her; Susan lived and scolded and kept a tight hand on everything. To her Daniel every Saturday brought the sum-total of his wages—sixteen shillings all told. Out of it Susan, always grudgingly, returned him sixpence for himself. It was enough, she said, for a man to spend on beer and tobacco in one week. Daniel took it thankfully. It represented an ounce of tobacco and three gills of ale—one on Saturday night, one on Tuesday night, one on Thursday night. Without the sixpence there would have been neither tobacco nor beer.

When Daniel found religion at the penitent bench in the little chapel, and was duly brought in as a convert, his financial position began to cause him some anxiety. His weekly sixpence was already laid out, but now there were new demands upon him. After studying the matter for a whole day he approached Susan.

'Thou mun let me hev a shillin' i'steeäd o'

sixpence now,' he said. 'Sixpence weeän't do i' t' future—I mun hev a shillin'.'

'Aw, mun tha?' said Susan. 'And for why, pray? I'm sewer sixpence a week's plenty, and aboon plenty, to lig out i' bacca and beer. Doster know 'at sixpence a week is six-and-twenty shillin' a year?'

'I doän't want it for neyther beer nor bacca,' said Daniel. 'But tha sees, I've fun religion, and I'm bahn to be a member o' t' class-meetin', and it's a penny a week, and then theer's t' collections an' all.'

'Aw, is there?' answered Susan. 'Weel, lad, I'm nooän bahn to pay for thi religion—if tha will be religious, tha mun pay for it thysen. Tha wor goin' on all reyt wi'out onny religion—I doän't knaw what tha wanted to chaänge for.'

Seeing that it was hopeless to extract more money from Susan, Daniel was perforce obliged to think things over again. Remembering the adage that two heads are better than one, he consulted Sister Simpkin, the class-leader, on the matter. They considered the matter deeply, and in the end came to a decision. Daniel gave up beer and tobacco—the latter a sore trial—and in future laid out his sixpence in this way: one penny was spent in sweet-stuff (to console him for the loss of his pipe), one penny was devoted to his ticket, and another to the missionaries, while the balance of threepence was stored up against collection days, or such times as the Lord should show need of it.

It was through his connection with the chapel that Daniel fell in love. He was accustomed to walk home from meeting with his fellow-members, and it not unfrequently happened that he and Sister Jones held such converse by the way as tended to give them a most favourable opinion of each other. Sister Jones was a little woman of some forty years, stunted, withered, and gnarled by a life of field-labour; but Daniel was no authority on good looks, and cared nothing about outward appearances. He was drawn to Sister Jones by the sympathy which she showed towards him. His mother and Susan were the only other women with whom he ever held much converse, and one was peevish and querulous, and the other hard and repellent. Sister Jones, in spite of her ill-favoured looks, was a cheery little body; it gave Daniel a sense of relief and pleasure to hear her talk. And, therefore, he looked and longed for a promised land.

One night, as he and Susan sat in the cottage, she mending some garment, and he sucking one of the sweets that atoned so poorly for his old clay pipe, Daniel dared to mention the thing that was uppermost in his mind.

'I 've been thinkin',' he said, ''at it wor time I gat wed.'

Susan dropped her needle and faced him, sore amazed.

'Thee—get—wed!' she exclaimed. 'Thee! And who 'd ivver be sich a fooil as to marry a poor shammackin' creeätur like thee?'

'Nah, then, hod thi noise!' said Daniel. 'Theer 's somebody 'at 'll hev me—I can do a bit o' courtin' as weel as onnybody.'

'Tha 'll drive me mad!' said Susan. 'T' idea o' thee gettin' wed, or goin' courtin', wi' a poor owd bed-ridden mother to keep! Tha owt to be 'shaämed o' thisen!'

Daniel glanced uneasily at the great four-poster in the corner, where the old woman lay asleep.

'Who's ta been makkin' up to?' asked Susan. 'I insist on tha tellin' me all abaht it.'

Daniel grew frightened.

'It's nowt,' he said; 'I wor nobbut thinkin' 'at me and 'Becca Jones 'ud get wed—that wor all.'

'And plenty!' exclaimed Susan. ''Becca Jones, indeed! There would be a bonny pair on ye. 'Becca Jones! But I'll larn her a lesson next time I set ees on her. Nah, then, dooän't thee go in for noa more cantrips o' that sort. Tha's plenty to do to keep thi owd mother and me.'

'Say no more about it,' said Daniel.

After that life pursued an even course so far as Daniel was concerned. Whether the days were fine or wet, whether he was ill or well, whether the wind whistled through his thin clothes or the sun beat fiercely on his unkempt head, he moved about the land in his now permanent occupation of shepherd. You saw him in winter wrapped up in an old sack, which served the purposes of an overcoat, plunged almost to the knees in wet and heavy clay, feeding his sheep with turnips, and exchanging chance remarks with whatever straggler, gamekeeper, tramp, or idler, chanced to pass his way. Week after week he carried his wage home to Susan, receiving his sixpence with thankfulness; Sunday after Sunday he went to the little chapel and kept his one eye fixed steadfastly on the preacher. And sometimes he went to see 'Becca Jones in her little cottage, but there was nothing more said between them as to love and marriage.

At the age of fifty and three, Daniel, having had his thin and time-worn garments soaked to the skin several days in succession, found himself one day so ill that rising from his miserable bed in the cottage garret was a physical impossibility. Susan went up the ladder and scolded him. Poor folk, said she, had no business to be badly. Daniel shook his head. He asked her to fetch the doctor to heal his body, and the class-leader to comfort his soul. Then Susan was afraid, and she descended the ladder to tell the invalid mother that trouble was afoot. The old woman wept and fretted, while Susan went down the village street in quest of help.

'Eh dear, eh dear!' sighed Daniel's mother.

'Childer 's a deeäl o' trubble—a deeäl o' trubble —sure-ly!'

Poor Daniel, however, was to trouble nobody any longer. Next morning he was dead. 'Becca Jones came to see his body, and a tear or two rolled upon his face from her withered cheeks. Hers, at any rate, of all the hearts he had known, was not absolutely without humanity.

PARTED

As the twilight gradually deepened into darkness the woman rose from her seat in front of the fire, and lighted an oil lamp that stood trimmed in the centre of the little deal table. Its faint light at first did no more than indicate the gathering gloom, but when she turned up the wick there came out of the shadows a picture of light and shade, which presented itself to the eye in sharp and definite outlines. The woman turned from the lamp to the fire, and looked about her. She lifted her hand to her mouth, and yawned wearily. From her lips her hand fell, as if instinctively, to the kettle on the hob. Her fingers closed round the handle, and she placed the kettle in the centre of the glowing coals.

A low tap sounded on the cottage door. The woman went across the red-tiled floor in response; but before her fingers touched the sneck the door opened, and a face showed itself against the darkness outside.

'Come in, Mrs. Catheram,' said the woman who had lighted the lamp. 'I wor just hopin' you'd come—it's nobbut dowly wark sittin' here.'

Mrs. Catheram came in—a diminutive figure in rusty black, whose lithe movements opposed themselves to the hundred wrinkles of the parchment face. She set down a black bundle on the deal table, and gave a quick glance round the little house.

'Why, joy,' she said whisperingly, 'why, it is weary waitin' for 'em to drop off, to be sure. But we mun bide the Lord's time, you know —ay, surely.'

She began to untie her bonnet-strings as she spoke. While her long, clawlike fingers busied themselves about her throat, her eyes again ran round the house. Beyond the table, half-hid in shadow, stood a quaint four-poster bedstead, from which the hangings and draperies had long since vanished. The contour of its white sheets and patchwork quilt was broken but faintly by the outlines of a human figure. On the pillow rested a human face—gaunt, fleshless, a high nose projecting above a sunken jaw, and rings of grey hair straying loose from a dingy night-cap. A hand lay outside the quilt, and the fingers plucked at the sheets unceasingly. Mrs. Catheram saw the fingers, and nodded her head. She looked round in the opposite direction. Behind her, on the other side of the hearth, an old man sat in a hooded chair, fast asleep. His head, snow-white, fell back in the angle of the hood; his hands, thick and gnarled as the roots of an oak, lay twitching on his knees. His mouth had fallen open as he slept, and revealed a solitary tooth, long and yellow, that bent outward, and compressed his nether lip. Over his wrinkled face there lay the grey stubble of a beard; round his neck a strip of red flannel was twisted loosely above the band of his coarse shirt. A stout stick rested between his knees, and as the little woman in rusty black glanced at him, he started uneasily in his sleep and laid his hand on it.

The younger woman took down a teapot, and dropped three spoonfuls of tea into it.

'I wor just goin' to hev a cup o' tea,' she said. I 'm fair stalled o' waitin' for t' owd lass to mak an end on 't. Sit you down, Mrs. Catheram, and we 'll hev a cup together. It 's nobbut cowd outside.'

Mrs. Catheram sat down near the fire. The younger woman busied herself with preparations, bringing out a teacake and butter from the cupboard, and putting the teapot to warm on the oven top. A cat sleeping on the hearth-rug woke, and saw signs of a meal, and purred complacently. Outside the wind rose and began to sob and sigh in the elm-trees.

'Ah, listen to yond,' said Mrs. Catheram. 'It 's a sign is that, Hannah. They 're comin' for her. I 've heerd 'em many a time. When Bob Jasper died—eh, they howled and wowled round his chamber windows that awful till it made me afeerd.'

'I hope they 'll wait till we 've hed a cup o' tea, at onny rate,' said Hannah. 'It 's ready—help yoursen, Mrs. Catheram.'

The rusty black woman poured out a cup of tea, and then looked at Hannah inquisitively.

'Is there a drop left i' t' little bottle, lass?' she inquired. 'Work like mine, you know'—she nodded in the direction of the bed—'maks you need some'at comfortin'!'

'I 'd clean forgotten,' said Hannah. She rose and produced a little black bottle from the cupboard. 'It 's rum,' she said. 'Sixpen'orth—our Jack fotched it thro' t' "Dog and Duck."'

While they sat eating and drinking, the figure on the bed stirred, and the gaunt jaw moved feebly.

'Josey!'

'He 's asleep,' said Hannah, moving over to the bedside. 'He 's hevin' a nap. Go to sleep agen ; it 'll do you good.' The old woman's eyes turned themselves vacantly towards the light.

'Aw,' she said. 'Aw—ay, I dersay, a nap 'll do him a power o' good. Who 's there?'

'It 's me, Mally,' said Mrs. Catheram. 'We 're sittin' wi' you—me and Hannah, just friendly like.'

'Aw,' said Mally feebly. 'Aw.' She looked wonderingly at both the women, and her fingers worked quicker at the sheets. 'Hev ye come to lay me out?' she asked suddenly.

'Nowt o' t' sort!' said the woman in rusty black. 'None o' yer fancies—go to sleep agen ; that 's a good soul.'

The old woman closed her eyes, and turned her head to the wall. Hannah stood by her for another moment before she went back to her seat at the fireside.

'She 's off ageëan,' said Hannah, sipping her tea. 'She 's been like that on and off all day; it 's cur'us how clear her mind is.'

'She 'll none be long, lass.' Mrs. Catheram poured out more tea and more rum. 'They 're offens very clear i' their minds just afore t' end. And hark at t' wind—how it 's wowling outside!'

'Well, I doant care how sooin it 's ower,' said Hannah. 'It 's poor wark nursin' them 'at doesn't belong to you. I 've been in here all t' day, and our Sarah Jane 's hed to see to things at home.'

'Why, lass, we mun do a bit o' summut to help, thou knows. It 's unfort'nate 'at Josey and Mally heen't onny childer o' their own to see to 'em.'

'I expect owd Josey 'll be droppin' off t' next,' said Hannah, glancing at the sleeping figure in the chair. 'He 's varry near past doin' owt for hissen. Ye 'll hev to come and lay him out next.'

'I expect to lay a good many out yet, lass,' said Mrs. Catheram calmly.

It 's wark 'at I shouldn't like,' observed

Hannah. 'You mun ha' seen a deal o' corpses i' your time.'

Mrs. Catheram drank off her tea and nodded, glancing at her black bundle.

'I hev, my lass, I hev. Corpuses o' all sorts and sizes, high and low, rich and poor. Theer wor precious little difference i' onny on 'em when they were dead,' she added reflectively.

The old woman on the bed stirred again.

'Josey!' she said. 'Josey!'

'He 's asleep, I tell you,' said Hannah.

'Aw.' She was silent again. The women at the fireside sat staring at the glow of the cinders. Presently the old woman spoke again.

'Me an' Josey 's been wed fower-and-fifty year,' she said. 'Fower-and-fifty year come Martlemas.'

'They owt to be stalled on each other bi now, then,' said Hannah in an undertone. 'Go to sleep wi' you,' she added, raising her voice.

'Let her be, lass,' said Mrs. Catheram. 'She 'll just drop off quiet. Eh, that wind!—it 's gettin' wilder nor iver.'

Hannah cleared away the tea-things. 'I 'll just run round and see if our Sarah Jane 's gotten her feyther's supper ready,' she said. 'Ye can do wi'out me a bit, now.'

'Go thy ways, lass,' said the layer-out. 'Theer 's nowt to do.'

She turned to the fire as Hannah left the cottage, and, drawing her chair closer to the grate, began to warm hands and knees at its ruddy glow. Now that there were no human voices to break in upon it, the silence within the little cottage was deep and intense. The old clock in the corner ticked gently, the old man in his hooded chair breathed with regular monotony, now and then a cinder fell from the bars into the ash-pan; but around these slight sounds the silence wrapped itself, and beyond the silence rose the pathetic sighing of the wind in the elms outside.

After a time the layer-out rose and went over to the bedside. The old woman seemed to sleep, and she turned away from her and resumed her place by the hearth. The little black bottle still stood on the table—she laid hands on it half-mechanically, and took the cork out and put the neck to her lips, shaking her head mournfully after each sip. For half an hour she sat thus, nursing the bottle between her hands, and rocking her thin body and wrinkled face over the fire.

A curious rattling sound from the bed roused her at last. She laid the bottle on the table and bent over the bed, holding the lamp in her hand. The rattling in the old woman's throat died away as the layer-out stood and looked at her.

'Sudden at last,' she said, setting the lamp down. 'I mun just run round and tell Hannah. Josey's sound asleep yet, I declare.'

She went out and closed the door after her. The wind swept in and sent the lamplight flaring up to the blackened rafters for a moment.

Josey woke with a start. He had been dreaming, and he had seen a vivid flash of lightning across his eyes. He lifted his head slowly and looked round him. Everything that he saw was familiar—the little house, the bed, the fireside, the lamp burning on the table. He leaned back again and yawned, and became wide awake.

'Mally!'

He called his wife's name gently. Then he leaned forward and listened. When a moment had gone by he grasped his stick, and, pulling himself to his feet, hobbled over the hearth-rug towards the bed. He bent down to the still figure and spoke again, and then began to fumble amongst the sheets for Mally's hand. His fingers touched her face, and suddenly his hand rested on her forehead as on something very cold. A cry escaped his lips as he turned to the door, through which the layer-out was entering with stealthy tread.

THE OMEN

BEFORE ever I rose from my bed that morning I knew that for me the end of the world was all but come. Through the long hours of the earlier night I had lain in my bed asleep, yet not asleep. There was no power of motion in me—twice, thrice, and once again I tried to lift my hand from the coverlet on which it lay, and found myself unable to stir even a finger. All about me hung the thick, stifling darkness, and it hurt me so that I longed to scream with pain. My tongue clicked drily against my teeth; the roof of my mouth was parched; my lips burnt themselves with their own feverish heat; I could not have cried or spoken had I seen a ghostly hand point a knife at my heart. There I lay, while the heart of the night throbbed and pulsated all around my bed,—longing to sleep, to move, to cry out my terror, and finding myself powerless. It was as if I had died and still inhabited my body: I was myself, and yet not myself. Thus I lay while the night passed, hearing, as one hears the sound of a signal-bell from far off on a misty sea, the chiming of the clock on the stairs. With the grey dawn the horror shifted, and for a while I slept, but presently the first glint of light crept up the counterpane and touched my face, and I woke and dressed, and shivered because of the nameless terrors of the night.

That was my wedding-day. I crossed over to the window and drew up the blinds and looked out. The rain was falling heavily over a grey landscape. In my croft the cattle had grouped themselves together beneath the trees; further away, beyond the Black Coppice, I saw my sheep huddling against the nets in the turnip-field. Underneath my window the garden lay cold, bare, desolate. The walks were clogged with new-fallen leaves, the lawns were dank and wet, and the hawthorn hedge, destitute enough of leaf, showed black and shining against the grey background of the moody sky. Everything reminded me of death rather than of life. Had there been a bird to sing one note of his song, or even a stray thrush to hop about my seed-beds, I might have forgotten myself and my thoughts—but the garden was lifeless, forsaken: it spoke to me of nothing but sadness and deep regret.

Upon the oak chest in the deep window-place lay my wedding finery. It had come home the night before, and the women had laid it there in order. I stood and gazed at it, and for the life of me I could not realise that it was mine, and that I was to wear it that day. I pictured myself in it, and laid a finger on the lace and the ruffles, and drew it away again as if I had touched some uncanny thing. But I put the various articles on one by one. When I came to the coat I took it in my hands, holding it by the shoulders, and so sat down on my bed, and began to stare fixedly at the steadily falling rain.

I was at that time thirty-six years of age, and all my life I had done my own will and pursued my own pleasure without let or hindrance. The land that I tilled was mine; mine were the old house and all its comforts; mine, too, the money that my fathers had toiled early and late to hoard. There was no man in the Riding that I had reason to envy—nay, there was none that I did envy until that day. But that morning, sitting there with the drip, drip, drip of the rain sounding in my ears and the meadows lying dank and dismal before my eyes, I envied the meanest labourer that toiled for me. It seemed to me then that poverty was a more enviable thing than great riches, for I knew poor men who were content. I was not.

Years before that, when I first became my own master and lorded it over my land and those that lived upon it with all the arrogance of a boy made sovereign over a kingdom, I had sinned. It was no common sin, but rather a sin which nothing can atone for, a sin that neither God nor man ought to forgive. I had cast my eyes on a girl in a neighbouring village, and from that moment she and I were lost. She loved me as a good woman will love a bad man, for in her heart there was no thought of wickedness—she was pure as the white blossom that comes on the hawthorn in later spring. For her love I gave her lust; for her faith, betrayal. I think the devil entered into and possessed me at that time. All the arts that wickedness can devise I used—and so at last my evil deeds came to their fulfilment, and for the happiness that she had dreamed of I gave her misery, tears, the portion of all who trust and are deceived. Even then I never felt any pity for her—she seemed to me no more than the flower which one picks by the wayside to delight one's senses for a moment, and then to fling away. When she died I was conscious of only one thought—that it was better to know her dead than living. 'The dead have no power to reproach,' I said, and I went about with a light heart.

It was strange that I never once thought of this passage in my life until the eve of my wedding-day. The years passed and I lived my life and prospered, and at last made up my mind to settle down and marry, and raise up children to fill the old homestead with happy-hearted laughter. I looked about me for a wife, and those who had a right to judge said that I chose wisely. Her father's land and mine marched together, and because she was an only child all his acres would some day be hers, and therefore mine. He and I were friends—we settled the marriage between us before ever I said a word of love to his daughter. I could never tell whether she loved me at any time or not. Her lips were cold when they met mine, and there was no responsive gleam in her eyes when I gazed at her. It was that coldness, I think, that made me love her so madly. She seemed something high, unapproachable, and because of it I grew to desire her as a man might desire an angel. I shook with emotion at the thought of losing her. Her seeming coldness stung me to a furious desire to take her to my heart and kiss her into warmth and throbbing life. There was not a pulse within me that did not beat for her, not a drop of my blood that did not turn to fire if she touched my hand.

Upon the eve of our wedding-day I left her in the gathering gloom of the October twilight, and rode homeward across the land in a gay good-humour. She had seemed less cold—nay, she had lifted her cheek for another farewell kiss as I turned from her to my horse's stirrup. I shouted a laughing farewell to her as I put my horse at the first hedge. When I had cleared it I turned in the saddle and looked back, and saw her at the orchard gate waving her hand in the gloom. I rode away mad with love. I laughed, I sang, I rushed my horse at the great hedges that shot out of the twilight to meet us, I yelled at the startled cattle in the meadows. And through all there rang a continual chiming in my heart that said, 'To-morrow! To-morrow! To-morrow!'

But in the twilight I came to a lonely churchyard in which that other woman's dead body lay lonely and cold in the damp, clinging earth. I drew rein and looked over the wall, and gazed at the corner in which they had buried her. It was a fearsome place—the nettles grew rank and thick everywhere, and the white mist seemed to hover like a ghost above them. I looked and looked again, and yet again—and it was then that the nameless horror came into my soul and filled it. I could have cried with terror as I shook the reins, but my tongue was dry and my teeth chattered. I began to shake as a man shakes in the ague. The horse tossed his head and moved on, and I clutched at the bow of the saddle to save myself from falling. The curse was upon me.

As I crossed the open down before my door, two black blots showed themselves against the light skyline between the horse's ears, and as they were lost in the wavering darkness I heard the cry of ravens.

After that I knew that it was in this life that I must begin the punishment of my great sin.

I thought over all these things as I sat by the bedside, holding my wedding-coat in my hand, and staring through the window at the dripping landscape outside. Nothing would lift the black horror from my soul, but at last I rose and finished my preparations, and went down the stairs to outward appearance as brave a bridegroom as any woman could desire. Through the steadily falling rain I rode, passing thorpe and hamlet as one rides by the ghostly imaginings of a dream, and at last I came to the church, and saw the wedding guests assembling at the door. It was not I, I think, but something which had usurped my place, that waited so long at the altar for the bride that came not. But it was I that at last rushed from the church and leapt upon my horse and rode away, throwing back great peals of mad laughter that echoed along the wondering street.

THE EVE OF THE WEDDING

DICK finished his tea-supper with a sigh of deep contentment. He smiled as he looked at the round of cold pressed beef that stood before him. There was something about its diminished size that seemed to appeal pathetically to the empty egg-shells which flanked it. Dick smiled again and lifted the teapot. He waved it at the pictures, as he had seen his mother do many a time, and then essayed to pour liquid from its black spout into his cup. But the teapot was empty; it seemed to groan as Dick set it down. Beef, eggs, tea—he had made an example of all, and the brown loaf of bread had suffered with them. For seven long September hours Dick had tasted neither bite nor sup, and he was therefore sharp-set when he came to table. He now left it, satisfied and happy.

Margery came into the parlour to clear away the tea-things. From beneath the depths of her white cap she gazed at the remnants of the feast. When she had duly noted the ruin of the plateful of eggs and the diminished proportions of the round of beef, she lifted the teapot and made a mental calculation as to its contents.

'Lord be good to us, master!' said Margery. 'For a man that contemplates holy matrimony on the morrow, your appetite is truly amazing! It did use to be said when I were a young maid—a long, long time ago, alack-a-day!—that to be in love meant to be without an appetite. But young folk are so different nowadays.'

Dick laughed. He had got his big frame into the old chair at the fireside by that time, and was settling down for half an hour's comfortable repose with pipe and tobacco.

'There's naught meddles with my appetite, nor yet my sleep, Margery,' said Dick. 'A man must eat if he means to work, mustn't he? Only with me the work usually comes before the eating, and that's why I'm always ready for what there is.'

'And a good job, too,' said Margery. 'Ay, indeed, a good job! I've known them 'at could neither eat nor yet sleep for love—ay, marry, I have so. So thank the Lord, lad, that it's not so wi' thee.'

'Thank the Lord!' said Dick somewhat irreverently. 'And what was it that made 'em like that, eh, Margery? For love, was it? Why, I'm in love as badly as a man can be——'

'Love,' said Margery, 'is a queer thing. But it was 'cause they were in love that they could neither eat nor sleep, sleep nor eat. But you're young, my lad, and what should you know of such things? It's been all love's pleasure wi' you, and none o' love's pains. Eh, well—I hope it's to be like that always, master. I'm getting old, and I could like to see thy boy on my knees before I go.'

'You shall dance at my boy's wedding, Margery,' laughed Dick. 'And that'll be something over twenty years to come, at any rate. Old?—why, you'll shake as loose a leg as any of them to-morrow, I'll be bound.'

The old woman laughed and went out with her tray, and Dick picked up the county newspaper and began to read over his pipe. But there was little in the paper to interest him, and he presently flung it aside. His thoughts turned to the morrow—the morrow that was to make him bridegroom to the sweetest girl in all the world. At the thought of her his heart beat quicker, his blood leapt in his veins, a great tide of happiness surged over his soul, his entire being seemed lifted up to heights of mysterious joy. To-morrow she was to be his—sweet Letty Gray, whose sunny hair and violet eyes had won his heart from the first. She had been hard to woo and harder still to win, but at last all barriers had been swept away before love's overwhelming tide, and on the morrow she was to give herself to him. He sat and thought of her, and of the great joy that was coming to him. And at last the old clock in the farm-house kitchen struck seven, and then Dick rose and knocked the ashes out of his pipe and left the house. He was going to meet Letty for the last time as her lover. That night they would meet and later on say good-bye—after the morrow there would be no parting between them.

Dick went slowly through the quiet village, sleeping softly in the light of the harvest moon. Like most lovers, he was early at the trysting-place. He sat on the old stile by the churchyard and waited, his eyes fixed on the path by which Letty must come to him. Everything was very quiet thereabouts—there was scarcely a sound from the village street, and the noise of the little stream beyond the Five-Ash Coppice came to his ears in a subdued murmur. It seemed to Dick that all things spoke of love and happiness—of love brought at last to full fruition, of happiness all the sweeter because it had been waited for. And then he caught sight of Letty's light dress coming through the thin belt of trees that wrapped the Mill-House in gloom, and he got down from the stile and went slowly to meet her.

They met by the old tree that stands in the centre of the Duke's Garth—an ancient oak that has doubtless heard the vows and whispered protestations of generations of lovers. Dick held out his hands. The girl slid her own into them, and held up her face.

'How cold your hands are, Letty!' said Dick, raising his head from her face. 'And your lips too. What's the matter, dear? You're not ill, Letty?'

Letty looked at him. He saw traces of tears

on her cheeks, and unshed tears showed themselves in her eyes. Dick put his arm about her. At that protecting touch the girl burst into tears.

'Letty!' Dick was genuinely alarmed. 'My dear love! What is it?'

She suddenly released herself from his arm, and leaned back against the tree, and looked at him.

'I'm not ill, Dick,' she said. 'But I'm unhappy and miserable.'

'Unhappy? Miserable?'

A strange, cold feeling surged over Dick's heart. It seemed to him that he had suddenly come into the presence of something which he could not understand. He stepped closer to the girl, and held out his hands again.

"It's not about to-morrow, Letty?' he said. 'For God's sake, say it isn't!'

She had been hard to win, hard even to woo, and even sometimes he had thought that the love was all on his side. His heart beat with anxiety as he stood watching her in the moonlight.

Letty bowed her head.

'Oh!' she sobbed, 'I can't help it, Dick, I

can't indeed. It is about to-morrow—because, Dick, I—I don't love you as I should do.'

Dick came close to her and possessed himself of her hands.

'Letty!' There was something of command in his voice now. 'Letty! Speak to me—tell me true, now. Is it because there 's some other—man?'

She nodded her head and sobbed afresh. Dick drew a long breath.

'Who is he?' he asked, feeling that the happiness of the night was suddenly turned into despair.

'He 's dead,' she answered. 'Dead—dead!'

She leaned her face against the tree and burst into a storm of bitter weeping. Dick stood close by, silent and full of wonder. He could say nothing and do nothing to relieve the girl's distress, but he was conscious of a great relief. Dead? Then he had no rival! In his heart he thanked God for that.

After a time he put out his hand and laid it gently on Letty's shoulder.

'Come, my dear,' he said, 'come, tell me all about it. Dear heart—it kills me to see you crying like that.'

Letty came closer to him, nestling almost against his broad shoulder.

'You're my true friend, Dick, as well as my lover, aren't you?' she said, looking at him appealingly.

'I am, Letty,' he answered. 'God knows I am!'

'I'm weak and silly, perhaps, to-night,' she said. 'And I've been unhappy this last week or two because I—well, I got thinking about—him, you know. It was before we came here to live, Dick, before you knew me—and—and—we did love each other true. And he had to go away, Dick, and he was—lost at sea. And oh, Dick—I was dreaming about him last night, and I saw him—alive!'

She shuddered convulsively, and her hands clutched Dick's arm as she looked fearfully into the white moonlight. Dick put his arm about her protectingly.

'Hush!' he said. 'You're a bit overwrought, Letty, and you're not well. So I wasn't the first wi' you, Letty?'

'No,' she whispered. 'Forgive me, Dick. I ought to have told you, but somehow I couldn't. And besides I liked you, Dick.'

'But you loved him,' he said.

'Yes,' she sighed. 'But he's dead. Was it wrong to think about him, Dick? I couldn't help it, I couldn't indeed!'

'No,' he answered. 'Of course you couldn't, my dear—no more than I could help thinking about you. But oh, Letty, this is sad news to me, for I love you, my lass, with all my heart, and I thought I'd won your love in return.'

Letty looked up at his face, and was moved by the pain which she saw there. She drew still closer to him and raised her face to his.

'I'll be a good wife to you, Dick,' she whispered.

'But your love's his,' he said. 'O Letty, it's awful! And I thought—I thought you loved me!'

He suddenly put her away from him, and stood looking at her in the moonlight. Letty began to weep again.

'I'm very sorry, Dick,' she said. 'I know I ought to have told you before, but it's hard to tell things like that, and besides he's dead—dead! And I will be a good wife, Dick; and, perhaps, I shall get to love you as I ought to.'

Dick shivered.

'Don't, Letty!' he said. 'Don't! My lass, I couldn't marry you without love.'

'But you do love me,' she said.

'And you don't love me,' he answered.

'I like you, Dick. You're the best man I know.'

'I'd rather I was the worst, if so be as you loved me,' he said. 'Good God, Letty, do you think I can take you into my arms, knowing that you haven't any love for me? There may be men that can do that—but I can't, Letty; I can't! It must be love, and no less.'

'Dick!' she said, 'Dick! I do love you. I've always loved you—in a way, you know, and I seem to love you better. It was only because I couldn't bear to marry you until I had told you all about that.'

Dick's heart leapt within him. He suddenly seized the girl in his arms and held her to him, showering sudden kisses over her lips and cheeks and forehead.

'Say that again!' he whispered. 'Tell me you love me again, Letty! Oh, my dear, you've told me all; now let's forget. Letty, Letty, it's more than liking that you have for me, isn't it? Say that it is, Letty; say that you love me!'

She would have been more than human if she had resisted the passion in Dick's voice and the kisses that fell upon her lips. She nestled close to his breast, and for a moment forgot everything but him.

'O Dick!' she sighed, a new feeling for him filling her heart. 'I believe I do—I believe I do!'

'But you love him?' he suddenly said, disengaging her arms from his neck, and looking searchingly into her face. 'You love him—yet?'

Letty bowed her head. The tears began to run down her cheeks again.

'I can't help it, Dick—I can't indeed,' she pleaded. 'If you'd only known——'

'Ah,' he said, 'if I'd only known!'

He still stood gazing at her. Letty began to be afraid.

'Oh, dear!' she said at last. 'What a puzzle it all is, isn't it, Dick? But we've got to make the best of it, haven't we? There, Dick, I wish I hadn't told you, but I felt I had to.'

She came to him and put her hand on his

arm. They walked across the meadow towards the garden gate of Letty's home.

Dick went back to his lonely hearth later in the evening. The lamp burnt brightly on the table, there was a clear fire in the grate, and on the little stand by the easy-chair old Margery had set out the materials for his one glass of grog. Dick had pictured to himself the difference which Letty's presence would make in his parlour. It was bright and comfortable enough, but it needed a woman's presence to make it feel like home. Woman and woman's love—Dick's heart had cried for both, and then rejoiced in finding them in Letty.

He thought of these things as he stood before the fire, looking down into the glowing flame. A woman's love!—he thought he had found it, and, lo! it had been another's all the time. Between himself and the woman he had chosen from all other women of his world there rose the apparition of the dead man. What had Death to do with Love and Life! What?—but Love had much to do with Life and Death, for it could endure through both. Death had no power over Love—had he not seen the tears drop from a woman's eyes because of her love for a dead man whom nothing, not even the great God Himself, could give back to her? And that woman was the woman whom he loved with the love which only comes once, and who could never give him the first, fresh love that he had desired and hoped to win.

He stood there, thinking. Old Margery's words came back to him with strange force—'It's been all love's pleasure wi' you, and none o' love's pains.' He laughed grimly at the thought. Pleasures? Ay, but they were imaginary. There had been vows of love and passion, kisses, the hundred and one tricks of lovers—and all the time there had been between himself and his promised bride the ghost of a dead man!

It was midnight when Dick turned away from the hearth. All that time he had never moved. The fire burnt low and went out; the red cinders turned to grey ashes, the lamp's light grew low; deep shadows filled the corners of the room. In the vaulted hall outside there were weird murmurs of the wind that swept along passage and corridor and made the casement shake and rattle. He climbed the stairs in the fitful moonlight and went into his room. He lighted a candle, and in its first gleam caught sight of his wedding finery laid out on the bed. He turned from it, and from all that it suggested, with a dead regret—between him and the dearest hopes of his heart there stood a grey spectre, which not even the morning light would charm from his sight.

HAGAR AND ISHMAEL

I

When the train began to roll and creak its sinuous way out of the little station there was no one on the narrow platform but the woman who had alighted and the collector who stood waiting to take her ticket. He leaned idly against the door of his office; she, lingering near the edge of the platform, looked out across the level landscape that ran up to the borders of the railway line opposite. It was a dull December morning; the sky was a mass of grey clouds, and there was a sobbing wind that seemed to threaten rain. The ticket-collector shivered, and wondered why the solitary figure in rusty black lingered staring at the dank meadows and mist-sodden woods. But when she turned he forgot the cold, raw air, and thought of naught else but her face, which was full of a tragic beauty such as he had never yet set eyes on. There was something in the face that awed and frightened while it attracted him, and he mechanically lifted his fingers to his cap as he took the third-class ticket which she held out to him.

As she was passing out of the station the woman turned and looked at the collector. Although she said nothing, he drew near, and again touched his cap. She glanced at him as a superior at an inferior—he felt, somehow, that her eyes expressed a gloomy pride. They were glowing eyes, burning in dark sockets, and thrown into fierceness by the excessive pallor of the brow and cheeks, and they frightened him. But he stood, waiting, sure that the woman was about to speak to him.

'There is a village named Fenton West near here?' she said interrogatively.

'Fenton West, ma'am? Yes, ma'am—about two miles along the road there,' he answered, finding it a great relief to speak at last. 'You can see the spire of the church just over the wood yonder.'

'And from there to Queen's Malbis—how far is that?' she said.

The ticket-collector considered distance. 'A good five miles,' he said. 'Yes, nearer six, I should say, ma'am. But there's a highroad all the way.'

The woman lingered for a second or two as if she meditated some further inquiry, but presently she turned abruptly away with a nod of thanks, and went across the station-yard towards the lane outside. The collector's eyes followed her until she disappeared from sight; then he retired within his office, and drew a deep breath of wonder as though he had just seen something that amazed him. He went out again in a few moments, and walked along the platform until he came to a point which commanded the long stretch of road. The woman he looked for was walking with quick steps along the pavement in the direction of Fenton West village.

There is in Fenton West an ancient school, endowed some three hundred years ago, the master of which is permitted to take into his own house a certain number of resident pupils. The school stands back from the village street, and is set in the middle of an ornamental garden; the master's house overlooks it. Into the garden walked the woman in black at the same moment which saw the boys released for their mid-morning playtime. She looked at none of them as they clustered about her. She went up to the door of the master's house and knocked. Once inside the little room where the master kept his books and papers, she sat down, stern-faced and very quiet, and did not even turn her head to glance at anything until the old man opened the door and stood before her.

'You have a boy in your charge named Richard Frere?' she said, making no response to the schoolmaster's greeting.

'Yes—I have,' he answered wonderingly.

'He has been here some time,' she said, looking round her, as if to examine Richard Frere's surroundings. 'It is, I think, ten years.'

'Ten years, madam,' said the master. 'When he came he was five years old—he is therefore now fifteen—a tall, fine boy,' he added, with some pride.

A swift look shot across the woman's face.

'I am his mother,' she said shortly. 'I am Mrs. Frere. I wish to see him.'

The old man looked up at her with a sudden interest.

'His mother!' he said wonderingly. 'I did not know — I have often wondered who it might be that——And you have never seen him for ten years!' he added, with increasing wonder.

'Will you bring him to me?' she said, sitting down again.

The old man went out. As he shambled across the garden to the school-house his thoughts went back to the day, ten years before, when a man brought little Richard Frere to him, and paid down a year's fees in advance for his board, lodging, and teaching. Every year since then had come a letter, written in a fine Italian hand, covering a draft for the next year's fees, and making formal inquiry after the boy's health and welfare. Beyond the signature, 'Margaret Frere,' there was nothing to show who the writer was. The schoolmaster had wondered and conjectured, but had never succeeded in fathoming the mystery which surrounded his young charge. It was perhaps because of it that he had taken a strong liking to Richard.

It seemed to him that the child was absolutely lonely—in all the ten years no one had asked for him at the school-house door; no one had shown any sign of affection for him. Save for the coldly formal letter that came every Easter, with its firm signature and slip of blue paper, there was nothing from the outside world to show that any one thought or cared for the lonely boy.

'His mother!' said the old man, drawing near to the boys in his playground. 'His mother! And for ten years—and maybe longer—she has never cared to see his face!'

Richard Frere was playing football. His face was flushed, his eyes sparkled with the exertion. When the master looked at him he had no doubt as to the identity of the woman in his study—the mother's face was the son's face. But there was one difference—the woman's hair was raven black, streaked with threads of white; the boy's was a bright chestnut brown, that tumbled in rings and curls all across his forehead.

The schoolmaster took Richard Frere into his parlour, and told him who it was that awaited him in the study. The lad began to tremble. He was tall and straight and strong, and had never known fear in his life, but at the thought of seeing some woman whom he must henceforth call by the name of mother a great concern fell upon him. He shrank behind the schoolmaster when the old man opened the study door. But the schoolmaster laid a kindly hand on his shoulder and pushed him forward. The black figure in the chair turned and looked at him.

'Madam,' said the old man, 'this is your son.'

The woman half-rose from the chair, her hands suddenly tightened on the arms, and she bent her face forward and looked at the boy with eyes that were lighted up with a wonderful eagerness. She looked at him up and down, from head to foot, from foot to head, and her gaze rested at last on the chestnut curls. With a quick gesture she rose and walked over to the window, and the old man's observant eyes saw her lift both hands towards her breast as if to repress some emotion that was rising there.

At last she turned. 'So you are my son,' she said, with calm self-command. 'You are a proper boy to look at, and I hope you are master of yourself. At last I have come to fetch you—you are to go away with me.'

'To go away!' The old man and the boy spoke together. 'To go away!'

'Certainly—that is why I came. Make yourself ready at once, boy—it is time that we were on our way now.'

'I trust he is to come back to me, ma'am?' said the old man, his hand trembling as it lay on the lad's shoulder. 'I hope——'

But the woman had turned to the window again. She made no answer to the master's question, and he, with a sense of curious fear at his heart, signed to the boy to leave the room and prepare himself for his journey. He himself remained, sore perplexed and full of wonder. He wished to ask many things, but when the woman turned to him again his first glance at her face showed him that it was useless to speak to her. He sat down and waited, while she, still standing, fixed her eyes on some imaginary point, and gazed steadily before her.

II

Nicodemus unlocked the west door of the church at Queen's Malbis, and stepped into the low, dark room under the tower. He took the mattock and shovel from his shoulder, and placed them against the wall. Then he unrolled his sleeves and put on his jacket, and, sitting down on the old oak chest, which was gradually rotting to pieces in the corner, he produced his tobacco-pipe and applied a lighted match to the shreds that were tightly plugged into the bottom of the bowl.

'Five minutes to twelve,' said Nicodemus, folding his arms and kicking one heel against the oak chest; 'and seeing that I 've worked like a heathen negro for five mortal hours, I contend that I 've a right to them five minutes. Lawfully, they 're the church's, seeing that I 'm a minister of that great establishment; but nobody gets or gives all that should be given and got, and therefore I shall take five minutes for myself. 'Taint lawful neither to smoke 'bacca in consecrated places; but seeing that this ancient chamber is as damp as old Squire's vault below the chancel, a pipe is allowable, in my opinion. There ought to be something short kept in this old chest. A drop of anything——'

Matthew pushed the door open and entered.

He was attired in his Sunday best, and looked spick and span. Nicodemus nodded to him.

'You're in good time,' said he. 'The burying isn't till two o'clock. I've only just finished the grave—they're bricking it now.'

'Parson said I was to start ringing at half-past twelve,' answered Matthew. '"Start at half-past twelve and ring every minute on the muffled bell until the funeral corteege is in the churchyard," says he. So here I am, and 'tis a monotonous task that lies before me.'

'Ay,' said Nicodemus, ''tis so. Not but what a man can do a good deal between one minute and another. For instance, he can smoke his pipe, or he can put his lips to a bottle-neck, such as that which sticks out of your pocket at this moment, neighbour.'

'Oh!' exclaimed Matthew, visibly disconcerted, and clapping his hands on the bottle. ''Tis a drop that I called in at the Crown for. Will you join me in a drink, neighbour?—'tis mortal cold in this tower.'

'Ah!' Nicodemus removed his lips from the bottle-neck. 'You were always a rare judge of good drink, Matthew, and your judgment hasn't failed you this time. I'll come up the ladder and have another drink out of your bottle when I come back.'

'Do, neighbour, do,' said Matthew, with evident fear. 'Though it's but a little bottle. Is it going to be a big funeral to-day, neighbour?'

'For some folks it would be called big,' replied Nicodemus. 'For some it would be termed small. Yes; a quiet affair, considering that the corpse is that of a great landlord and a baronet. Just the family and so on.'

'Well, we must all die.' Matthew sighed profoundly. 'Rich or poor, it comes to us. Last week it was old granny Wickfield; to-day it's the great Sir Richard. All his wealth, you see, didn't save him. At the age of forty years he dies, and his land and his riches and all his possessions is taken from him. Truly all flesh is grass, neighbour,' said Matthew, mechanically carrying the bottle to his lips.

'Ay,' said Nicodemus, 'so it is. Well, I never cared much about Sir Richard. His father was one of the fine old sort, and when he died the burying was as proper a one as you might desire to see. There was hatchments and mutes, and everybody in deep mourning, and they said there was as much crape and stuff as would have covered the churchyard. And there was ale too—gallons and hogsheads of it—and bread and cheese in the Tithe Barn. But them days,' added Nicodemus, 'is gone.'

'He was a fine figure of a man, though, was Sir Richard,' said Matthew, 'and looked uncommon well in his pink coat.'

'As good-looking a man as ever I saw,' said Nicodemus impartially. 'And yet no better for it. There was them that wasn't any better for it, too.'

'Ay,' said Matthew, 'so I've heard. There was some talk of him and that handsome daughter of old steward Green's, wasn't there, neighbour?'

Nicodemus shook his head.

'No more than was true, Matthew, my lad. A deal o' sins to answer for has Sir Richard, baronet though a' be. Ay, a fine-looking lass was Margaret—held herself up like a queen. 'Twas a poor come-out for her.'

'Well,' said Matthew, 'he's done wi' it now, neighbour. Good or bad, rich or poor, they don't come out of the grave when once they've entered it.'

'Not when I've dug it and Dick Smith's bricked it,' answered Nicodemus. He knocked the ashes out of his pipe, and got down from the oak chest. 'I'll away and have my bit of dinner, and make ready for clerking,' he added. 'When I come back, neighbour, I'll drink with you again.'

'And welcome, neighbour,' said Matthew hastily, 'if there's any left.'

Nicodemus went along the village street towards his cottage. When he came out again, an hour later, the people were flocking to the churchyard, and Matthew's muffled bell was sending its dull note across the grey landscape. Nicodemus had put on his Sunday clothes of sober black, and with them his most solemn air. He felt full of decorous sobriety and clerkly virtue, and said to himself that the office of clerk was more to his taste than that of sexton. To say 'Amen' in the reading-desk was better than to dig graves in the churchyard.

There were scores of people clustered about the porch and the tower when Nicodemus walked up. The church at Queen's Malbis stands on a slight elevation, and those who waited in the churchyard could see the funeral approaching along the winding highroad beneath. It drew nearer and nearer, and at last the vicar, with Nicodemus in attendance, went down the path to the lych-gate, and they began to carry up the dead man towards his grave. It was then that the woman and the boy drew near. She held him by the hand, and drew him away to the three yew-trees which stand in one corner of the churchyard. There they stood, waiting in silence, until the procession came out of the church again. The woman tightened her hold on the boy's hand. She looked across the graves, to a slight figure that followed the coffin as chief mourner—the figure of a boy of twelve or thirteen, blue-eyed, gentle-faced, with hair that exactly resembled that of the lad at her side.

'That's t' young heir,' said an old woman who leaned against the yew-tree. 'Young Sir Walter they'll call him now. Eh, dear, to think 'at a lad like that should hev all that land and money!'

The woman tightened her grasp on the boy's hand. He looked at her inquisitively, and, seeing her eyes fixed on the slight figure, he turned his own in the same direction, and watched the ceremony to the end. He was full of wonder, but there was something in his mother's face that made him refrain from asking questions, and so he stood there giving back silence for her silence.

At last the service was over, and Nicodemus's final 'Amen' sounded hollow and ghostly across the open grave. The assembled crowd began to melt away, going by twos and threes, and at last there was no one in the churchyard but Nicodemus and Matthew, busy at the graveside, and the woman and the boy. The two men, their Sunday coats off, and their trousers rolled up, looked at each other as each stuck his shovel into the soft earth.

'Shall we have an odd glass first?' said Matthew. ''Tis perishin' cold, and I can see a good fire at the Crown.'

'Agreed, neighbour,' said Nicodemus. 'He'll take no harm for half an hour.'

When they had gone, the woman took the boy's hand and led him up to the graveside. They stood looking at the coffin. The boy stared at his mother, and was afraid of her eyes. At last she spoke.

'See, boy,' she said, 'you asked me why I brought you here. I wished you to see this man buried. You see all this land, these wide meadows: you saw the great house that they carried him from? It was all his—he was a great man and rich. You saw the boy that followed him to this grave?—all the land and money are his now. And all should have been —yours. Richard, you are standing by your father's grave!'

The boy started back and looked at her. He suddenly comprehended all that she meant, and a great flush of colour spread over his face. He stared at the coffin, and from the plate on its broad top to his mother. Suddenly his heart burst, and with a great cry he threw himself into her arms.

'Mother! mother! mother!' he cried. 'O mother!'

Something woke in the woman's breast. Till then her heart had been all ice and stone; at the touch of the young arms about her neck she suddenly felt a glow of new fire wake within her, and with a sob she drew the boy to her, and let him sob his grief out against her breast.

LUKE'S LOVE

WHEN Dick Marrish came back to the village after his seven years' service in the army, there were not wanting those who said that his coming would do no good to somebody. He was a fine figure of a man, and wore his clothes with a rakish air that had its influence on the young women. He had seen many men and places during those seven years, and he had learnt to talk of his adventures and experiences in a fashion that made him popular in the parlour of the Brown Cow or round the farm-house fires. It was said that he had killed more than one enemy, though he never mentioned the matter himself. Neither did he mention anything of the wound which had left a scar across his left cheek. Some of the women said he was ashamed of the scar, because he was vain of his beauty; but the girls, who admired him not a little, considered the scar to add to his good looks. To them it was an ever-present proof of his bravery and heroism. In imagination they saw him doing great things, and thus each made a soft corner for him in her heart. The other men of the village knew that, and resented it: had it been possible, they would have sent Dick to the right-about without ceremony. He placed them at a disadvantage, and there was only one of them that did not feel jealous if he saw the ex-dragoon in company with the village maidens.

Luke felt no jealousy of Dick or anybody else. He was one of those simple-minded giants who trust everything and everybody, and since Lucy had promised to marry him he had believed in human nature and the world with added conviction. All his life he had loved her with that unselfish love which only a great heart can feel. It had been a dumb love —Luke had no gift of speech. His part was to love and feel in silence. He made no demonstration; he was happy if, at the end of a long day's work on the land, he could sit and look at Lucy, busied with needlework or knitting. Now and then he would approach her timidly, and let his toil-worn hand stray over her sunny head. When he stooped from his great height to kiss her, and caught the gleam of her eyes and the dewy freshness of her lips in one impression, Luke's head swam, and he experienced all the madness of a pure intoxication. He was almost afraid of those moments; they seemed to him the high festival days of life, and the remembrance of one of them was sufficient to keep him in a dumb content until the next came. 'As well have a stick for a sweetheart!' said the other girls with whom Lucy exchanged confidences. 'He's a strange lover that's satisfied wi' one kiss.' But Luke knew naught of that—he was filled with quiet happiness, and went about his work, beaming satisfaction on everybody, and dreaming, so far as his practical nature would let him, of the happy days to be.

As for doubts, jealousies, suspicions, Luke had no thought of them. Being true-hearted himself, he was naturally incapable of harbouring a wrong thought of others, and especially of the woman whom he had loved ever since he and she, boy and girl, trotted side by side along the lanes to school. But other folk whose eyes were sharper saw things which he could not see. They wagged their heads over ale-pot and tea-cup, and said to one another that Luke had best look after his sweetheart. It was easy to see, they observed, that Dick had made an impression in a certain quarter. And therewith they proceeded to discuss the matter from all points of view, and were glad of the diversion.

It was old Reuben Gledd that took upon himself the duty of speaking warningly to Luke. They met on a May morning in a deep-banked lane, topped with the first bloom of the hawthorns, and ankle-deep with the luxurious bursting of the grass. Reuben pulled up his pony, and stared at Luke from between its cocked ears.

'Thou 'rt nobbut a lad,' said old Reuben, 'and thou 'rt a good lad. I 'll gi' thee a word o' good counsel. Tak care of all 'at tha hes.'

Luke smiled broadly. He had been taught prudence and economy from his childhood, and never spent a sixpence where a penny would do as well. As to taking care of what he already possessed, he had always done that, and meant to continue doing it.

'I think you can trust me on that score, Mester Gledd,' he answered. 'I look efter mi own pretty weel.'

'There 's summat 'at thou isn't lookin' efter just now,' said old Reuben.

'Aw?' Luke stared. He looked round at his fields, as if to discover some sin of omission or commission detected by the old farmer's sharp eye. 'Aw? I dooänt know——' he began.

'It 's neyther crop nor cow, turnip nor tatey,' said old Gledd. 'I 'll warrant thee to look after them all reyt. It 's thi sweetheart.'

Luke's broad face flushed a sudden red. His blue eyes shot a glance of fiery interrogation at the old man. Reuben nodded his head.

'Now, then, tak a word o' counsel,' said he. 'There 's happen no harm done, but thee watch yon Dick Marrish. Sin' he came home to farm his mother's land he 's setten hafe the wenches crazy wi' his fine airs. Now, look efter thi own, mi lad. I 'm tellin' thee.'

Reuben touched up his pony and went forward, his old hat grazing the trailing clouds of hawthorn blossom. Luke stood and gazed after him until man and pony disappeared

Then he turned in the opposite direction, and went straight across the fields towards Lucy's house. There was no feeling of resentment in him—all that he was conscious of was a vague pain. He had no doubt of Lucy—how could he doubt the candour of her eyes?—but it hurt him to think that others dared to suspect her. And Dick Marrish—why, Dick was an old friend!

Half a mile from the house he met Lucy's father. The old man called to him from behind a hedgerow, and beckoned him to approach.

'I wanted to see thee, my lad,' he said. 'I'm a bit uncomfortable like about Lucy and yon Dick Marrish. 'Od-rabbit the wenches, they're as soft as soap ower Dick! I think if I were thee, I should aim at hastenin' t' weddin', lad.'

'What's it all mean?' said Luke hoarsely.

'Nay, I darsay it's nowt, lad, but he's been about t' place a good deeäl lately wi' his fine airs and graces, and he walked her home thro' t' church t' other Sunday neet, and I see'd 'em down i' t' Low Meadow together yesterday efter-noon. I telled her mi mind about it last neet, but she laughed it off, tha knaws, lad—said it wor a pity if a lass couldn't speak to an owd friend.'

Luke continued to stare at Lucy's father. His own mind was so far a blank, but across it there began to steal a cloud of curious emotion.

'Thou mun get her to put t' day forrard, lad,' said Lucy's father. 'And thou mun mak love to her a bit fiercer—lasses likes it hot and strong, thou knows.'

Luke glared at him, and said nothing. Suddenly he turned away, and went along the fields again. He saw the red roof of Lucy's house above the tree-tops. Until then the sight of it had always given him a thrill of pleasure. As he went about his own land it was his custom to look across country and let his eyes rest for a moment on the roof which sheltered his sweetheart. But now there was no pleasure in it—instead there was a dull pain that bit and gnawed at his heart. He dropped his eyes and walked forward, vividly conscious of the sunlight, the singing of birds, the white-topped hedgerows, the daisies and buttercups at his feet, the patch of celandine under the elm-tree, and yet still more conscious of an undefinable something that crushed his heart and suffocated him.

At last he stood on the doorstep of the house. The door was closed. He hesitated as he opened it. A fear came upon him lest Lucy should see the trouble in his face. He could picture her astonishment on seeing him there at that hour—the sudden interrogative arch of her eyebrow, the smile that would bring out the dimple in her cheek, the clear voice that would ask what he was doing there. His face cleared as these things came into his mind, and he opened the door and walked in.

There was no one in the kitchen. The old clock ticked by the wall, a cat purred contentedly on the hearth-rug, a score of buzzing flies made monotonous music in the window-place; but there was no sign of human presence. Luke stood against the dresser, listening. He was going forward to the stairs to call his sweetheart's name, when he suddenly caught the sound of Lucy's voice. It was not words, but laughter, that he caught, and there was something in the laughter that he had never heard before.

Lucy was in the dairy—a great cool place at the end of a long dark passage leading from the kitchen. Luke went down the passage.

Something had filled him with a great fear. What was that strange new note in the girl's laughter? It frightened him—his heart throbbed and his breath came in gasps, and he felt as if his emotion would choke him. And all the time he knew that he was afraid because he did not know what it was that he was afraid of.

The door of the dairy had a square of wire let into its top panel, and through this Luke's glance passed as he came to the end of the passage. Again he was vividly conscious of all his surroundings. He smelt the fresh butter, he saw the half-light of the cool dairy, he noticed the drip, drip, drip of the butter-milk still running from the churn; he recognised the dampness of the passage wall on which his right hand rested. And, above all these things, he saw Lucy, in her print gown, with its sleeves rolled above the elbow, leaning against the big stone table, with Dick at her side, his arm about her waist, his hand lifting her face towards his own. He saw the sudden flush of colour in her cheek and the quiver of her lips as they were turned to Dick's——

He went quietly back into the kitchen after five minutes had gone. His face was white as the hearth-stone by which he stood, and his eyes had fallen deep into their sockets. But now the suffocation at his heart and throat had passed away, and he breathed freely; and his hands were steady as he took down the gun that hung, ready loaded, over the fire-place. He strode gently to the door, and went out into the quiet garden. The sunlight flooded the grass, but beneath the lilac-bush lay a patch of black shadow.

THE ACT OF GOD

STEPHEN THORPE rose from his bed in the early morning, and lighted the candle on his dressing-table. He stared at his face in the glass, and saw sunken eyes set in dark circles, and chin covered with the thick stubble of a two-days' beard, lines and wrinkles that told of conflicting passions and emotions; and over all a general air of fierce soul-hunger. At any other time it would have made him afraid to see such a reflection of his own countenance, but he had no time for fear that morning. All night long he had tossed and turned in his bed. The clock on the stairs had kept up a monotonous ticking throughout the dark hours. It chimed one, and two, and three, and four, and five, and six between Stephen's downlying and uprising, and he counted the strokes every time. It was now half-past six, and the farmstead was astir. He drew the curtain aside, and looked out of the window into the fold. The winter morning was black, but over the granary roof the stars still burnt with the sparkling light that tells of frost in the air. He saw lights in the stables, and heard the heavy thud of the horses' feet as they crossed the straw-strewn fold to drink at the trough. From the kitchen beneath his chamber he caught the sound of the maids' voices, sleepy and irritable. There was a rattling of fireirons against the grate, the musical tinkle of the cinders as they fell on the hearth, the grating of a hob-nailed boot on the step as a man went in or out—he heard all this with a vague consciousness of having heard it a thousand times before, and yet never with such a feeling as that which was beating itself against his side.

'An hour and a half,' said Stephen Thorpe, as he turned from the window and began to huddle his garments upon him. 'One hour and half an hour—ninety minutes—five thousand four hundred seconds—and then he dies! I can see him now—he sits in the cell with two warders watching him—they have waked him up from his last sleep—and he is just realising that in ninety minutes he will die.

The parson has come to pray with him, and they are bringing his last breakfast. It is all last with him. He has slept for the last time, prayed for the last time, eaten and drunk for the last time, seen the light for the last time, looked at men's faces for the last time—and then he dies. Only ninety minutes! — they are going fast enough with him, no doubt, but they go slow, slow for me. And that's natural, for he's going to die—at eight o'clock exactly it will take place—whereas I'm going to live and possess the things that he cheated me of. After all, what's his agony to the agony that I've gone through because of him? Naught!'

Then he cursed the man who was about to die with a fierce hatred, feeling nothing of pity for him. And that done, he continued to dress, and while he dressed he let his mind go back to the things that had been.

It was Michael Lynford who lay in Grandchester Gaol waiting the hangman's summons, and Stephen hated and cursed him because in the days gone by they had been rivals. They were both men of a fierce nature, both intent on living and loving in their own way, and it was an ill matter for both that they fixed their affections on the same woman. Worse still was it that for many a day the woman seemed not to know her own mind. She was one of those who think it a fine thing to have more than one string to a bow, and it pleased her weak nature to see two men in love with her. To-day she encouraged Michael; to-morrow Stephen. Had they told each other all they knew, both had torn the thought of her out of their hearts and spat in disgust of her memory. But she was careful not to play off one against the other—it was only when she was alone with Michael that she showed Michael her heart—it was only when she and Stephen had their time to themselves that Stephen was made to believe she cared for him. Thus it came about that when she finally decided to marry Michael, Stephen swore a great oath that he would never more believe in either God or man. And one stormy scene he had with Michael's wife, in which he made her weep because of the fierce contempt with which he treated her, but it had been better for him if it had never taken place. For Michael's wife, like all of her sort, was a liar from the beginning, and she gave Stephen to understand that she had been entrapped into marrying his rival, and hinted darkly that Michael had poisoned the mind of her father against Stephen. After that Stephen hated Michael with a bitter hatred that never slept; but, having a sense of honour strong within him, he kept away from Michael's wife, though he loved her as fiercely as ever. Strong in all else, he was weak enough to believe in her, and there was not a day nor a night that he did not curse the fate that had given her to another.

Michael had been married two years, and during that time he and Stephen had never met on the old terms of friendship which once existed between them. If they crossed each other's path, it was in a sullen silence; if Michael entered inn or parlour where Stephen sat, he went out; if Stephen found Michael in the market-place and at the church door, he straightway went elsewhere. Thus from friendship they were turned to enmity. At first Michael wondered at it, for he knew no reason why Stephen should hate him. Once he stopped his old friend on the highway-side and asked him straightforwardly of the matter.

'Why,' said Michael, 'should we be enemies, Stephen? 'Tis true that I have won the girl that we both desired, but I won her fairly. You had equal chance with myself, but you lost the game. Is that any reason for the hatred you show me? I think not.'

Now, if the woman, Michael's wife, had been aught but a liar, all had been well. But she had already lied to Stephen, and he had believed her, and so he answered Michael with a curse and flung away, and after that there was no more speech between them at any time.

Stephen had sworn to be revenged. 'No matter,' said he, 'how long I wait, at last I will have my knife in his heart. It is poor work, this waiting, but my satisfaction will be all the greater because I have had to wait for it. Sooner or later I shall be amply revenged.'

It was at the end of the second year that Stephen's opportunity came. Upon a September afternoon the gamekeeper was found in the Home Spinney, shot through the heart.

When Stephen heard it, he remembered that he had seen Michael Lynford hurrying away from the Spinney that morning with his fowling-piece over his shoulder. That alone was sufficient to hang Michael, for between him and the dead man there had been a great enmity.

Michael had suffered serious loss because of the depredation of foxes upon his fowls, and when he failed to get suitable compensation for the damage sustained, he made up his mind to shoot every fox he saw. And that was all very well so long as his war upon the foxes was carried on secretly, but one day the game-keeper had found him dragging a fox which he had just shot into cover, and after that Michael was made to feel the enormity of his crime. The squire and the steward had delivered their minds to him, with threat and expostulation, and the followers of the hunt had ignored his greeting as they passed him on the road. Michael resented it, and even as Stephen had vowed vengeance on him, so he vowed vengeance on the keeper. And so there was naught wanting but Stephen's testimony to make the chain of evidence complete against him when Michael was charged with murder.

For a moment Stephen hesitated. All that he could say was that he had seen Michael crossing the field outside the Spinney with his gun on his shoulder an hour or two before the keeper's dead body was found. He knew that that in itself was naught—a thousand good reasons might be found why Michael's presence there was innocent enough. But he also knew that his evidence was sufficient to hang Michael. There was the dead man, shot through the heart, and Michael had been seen near the place with his gun, and it was known that he had vowed vengeance on him. It was enough, and Stephen knew it was enough.

'Guilty or innocent,' said he, 'he shall die. After all, it will only be his deserts for robbing me of the woman I loved.'

After that his heart never softened. He gave information and saw Michael arrested, and, when the trial came on at the Assizes, he repeated the story he had told before coroner and magistrates. And he heard his old rival sentenced to death, and his heart bounded to hear it. But when the judge had finished speaking, Michael turned to the man who had given evidence against him, and fixed him with a look.

'Stephen Thorpe,' he said, 'you have sworn my life away, and yet you have said nothing that wasn't true. But in your heart you know that I am incapable of murdering any man. Before God, I am innocent of this crime—and

I never had a wrong thought of you in my life, Stephen Thorpe, enemy as you are.'

Then they took him away, and Stephen mixed with the crowd and went homeward. Somehow there was something in Michael's voice and look that made him afraid, but he cursed his fears and hardened his heart, and looked forward to the day that should see Michael's shameful death. Once his rival was dead, the future seemed clear to Stephen.

And so at last the day had come. It was a dark winter morning, and Michael was to die; and Stephen rose and dressed with the intention of riding across the land until he came in sight of the tower of Grandchester Castle. He knew of a spot where he could stand until the black flag floated out against the grey sky. After he had seen that he would go home content.

The dawn was breaking as Stephen went down to the great kitchen. His breakfast was laid ready on the round table by the fireside, but on that morning he had no appetite. He poured out his coffee with a shaking hand, and fetched the brandy from the parlour cupboard and added it to the coffee in generous quantity. It seemed to give him new strength, and so he took more, and more again. And at last he put on his boots and spurs, and went out and saddled and bridled his horse, and rode away across the fields in the direction of the city. As he went the dawn widened. The sky was streaked with red and yellow, the trees and woods came out of the grey shadows of the dying night, across the grass there lay a subtle tint of silvery frost. Stephen saw these things, and did not see them; his eyes were bent over his horse's ears, fixed on the spot where the towers and roofs of Grandchester Castle would presently emerge from the misty light.

It was within five minutes of eight when he drew rein on the summit of a low hill. He backed his horse under the leafless branches of a solitary elm. He had often kept tryst there with the woman who in a few minutes was to be Michael's widow, and he remembered it now with a savage joy. Michael had robbed him: now Michael in his turn was to be robbed of all that he had. And he, he had been the instrument, the means of vengeance!

He took out his watch, and, letting the reins fall on his horse's neck, looked from its face to the grey tower across the hill. He could see the flagstaff, and he fancied he could hear the tolling of the bell. There were but two minutes to elapse. His heart beat itself with remorseless violence against his side as he watched.

'The hangman has got him!' he said. 'He is strapping his legs and his arms—he will never use either again. Now they are leaving the cell—the parson is praying—you have only a short minute, Michael Lynford. Look your last, Michael—see, there's the winter sun peeping over the prison wall. You'll never see his face again. Take your last look at all the sweet earth that I'm still living in—There, the hangman's drawn the cap over—Ah!——'

A dot of black, vague, indistinct, but clear enough to Stephen's eyes, shot up the flagstaff, and suddenly expanded, a square of awful darkness against the red-and-grey of the sky. He stared and stared, and something in his brain seemed to burst as he still leaned forward, staring. He grasped blindly at the saddle before he fell forward with a choking cry, half-smothered ere it reached his lips. Then his great weight dragged itself free of the saddle, and he fell to the ground, and lay there face downward with one arm outstretched to clutch the wet soil.

The horse bent its head and cropped the starved grass at the foot of the tree. It wandered by the hedge-side for five minutes, but at last it came back and put down its nose to the dead man's face. When it lifted its head again it looked round, and sent a long whinny of brute despair across the desolate landscape.

THE BEATIFIC VISION

JOHNNY sat in the sunlight, his eyes wearily blinking at a scant patch of shadow that lay over the dusty grass of the wayside. He had sat there in his shabby rocking-chair every fine day for some twenty years. To folks with the usual amount of brains, the years would have seemed long, dreary, and of an exceeding monotony. But Johnny, being a poor simpleton from his birth upward, scarce knew the difference between day and night. Early in the fine mornings his mother dressed him (using his father's cast-off garments for the purpose), fed him (as babies are fed), and set him in his chair outside the cottage door. There he flourished, like a cabbage or cauliflower, drinking in sunlight and fresh air. In the opinion of his rural neighbours it had been better if Johnny had never been born, and a merciful deliverance if Providence would only take him.

Whether Johnny had any thoughts of his own upon these points who shall say? The fact remains that he lived a life of great vegetable luxury, positively flourishing in the sun, and making up in summer for the privations of winter. From April until October he lived outside the cottage; from October until April his seat was near the fire. Summer suited him best; it was his great recuperator, and he fattened on it. Johnny's mother put her head out of the door and looked at him. Johnny grinned broadly—it was the only form of expression that he had. Sometimes, if strongly moved, he would give vent to his feelings by making a curious boo-ing sound, but for ordinary events the broad grin served. A stranger passing along the street might easily have taken him to be a perfectly sane person, for his smile was intelligent and his face attractive. It was only when you looked at his big blue eyes and saw the hopeless vacancy behind them, fixed in an unmeaning stare that never varied, that you saw Johnny in stern reality. Then perhaps you looked more closely and noticed his legs, dangling loose from his chair, and betraying a disposition to wander and wobble, or his fingers that played feebly with his stick—and then you knew him to be one of those beings who come into the world soulless.

When Johnny's mother's face withdrew, Johnny yawned and moved his head from one side to the other. He looked up the street; he looked down the street. His face wore the expression which you may see a thousand times a day in Bond Street—the expression of the utterly bored lounger who looks at what he has seen a million times before. Up the street—the mill, its sails going round, round, round, round, round, round, round; the Gaping Goose, its sign swinging in the light breeze; the school-house, its weathercock glittering in the sun; a row of cottages; the gables and roofs of a farmstead. Down the street—the rookery, with the young rooks risking their half-feathered necks at the edge of the nests; the towers of the Manor rising through the trees; the church spire; the village green, and the little pond that flashed in the sunlight. Johnny looked—up, down—up, down—and rubbed his nose in sheer vacuous unconcern. He had seen all these things a thousand times and ten thousand upon that. They were the extreme limits of his world. In his twenty years he had never travelled even as far as the duck-pond or the mill. There was a vague notion somewhere in his body that something lay beyond his little circle of vision, but he had no power to wonder what it might be. He fell back upon his favourite amusement of grinning at the shadows on the grass.

When Johnny next looked up the street, he saw rare things approaching. Over the crest of the hill came a great company such as his eyes had never seen before. It came like a cloud at first, and, growing larger, assumed the proportions of a great procession. Johnny began to feel a tender interest in this thing that moved steadily towards him. Never in his life had he seen aught like it. He was always interested in the passing of a horse, and sometimes he had seen a little procession of four stone-wagons go by, and had boo-ed at them for pure delight. But this—why, already the advance-guard was abreast of the Gaping Goose, and still there were things coming over the hill-top half a mile beyond. Johnny looked, and looked, and at last lifted up his voice in one long, deep howl of joy.

'Boo—oo—oo—oo!' said Johnny.

Johnny's mother ran out of the cottage; her neighbour appeared at the next door. They stared up the street, urged thereto by the vigorous waving of Johnny's right arm.

'It's t' circus folk,' said the neighbour. 'They're bound to Cornchester. Sitha, Johnny!'

But Johnny needed no admonition. He gazed, and gazed, and gazed again. His blue eyes were big as saucers: his mouth stood agape. He saw rare things, and did not comprehend anything but that they were exceeding rare.

First there appeared men, riding in a gorgeous car drawn by many horses—black, brown, white, and piebald. The horses had exceeding long tails, and the men applied hands and mouths to shining things out of which came a divine music. The sound echoed and rang through the village. The schoolmaster and his flock appeared at the schoolhouse door; the farmers' wives peeped out of the windows, and their daughters ran to the gates; the parson looked over his hedge, and the blacksmith came out of the forge; the geese by the pond rejoiced loudly, and the dogs that lay sleeping in the sun woke up and barked. Then Johnny's mouth relaxed, and he joined the chorus.

'Boo—oo—oo! Boo—boo—boo!' cried Johnny.

But now came wonderful matters. Great beasts walked solemnly by whose tails hung from between their eyes, and whose tread shook the little houses. They bore gorgeous things in scarlet and gold upon their backs, and in one of them rode a great man, with a shining crown upon his head and a flashing sword in his hand. Johnny's mouth widened to a perfect O. But then followed other marvels. Beasts passed before him whose backs were fashioned with great humps, and whose feet trod softly in the powdery dust. A milk-white steed bore a black man, whose glittering teeth made Johnny afraid until a beautiful lady with wings on her shoulders came by and smiled at him. Little cows, with crumpled horns, drew a tiny carriage; a beast with rings all over it was led by a beautiful gentleman in green and gold.

And then came birds, great white birds, with long necks and legs, whose snowy plumage glittered in the sun. Houses on wheels, with wonderful pictures on the sides, passed by. In some of them were awful beasts that howled and roared and made Johnny afraid. But ere he had time to whimper came a company of merry gentlemen whose faces were painted in white and red, and whose clothes made Johnny think of the hangings round his grandmother's bed. He boo-ed with delight, and they smiled at him and cut an antic or two for his special benefit. And then came more solemn beasts, with their misplaced tails waving from side to side, and upon the head of one of them rode a curious little animal that wore a scarlet uniform, and mopped and mowed at the people; and so there was an end of it all, and Johnny sat staring at the last elephant as it wound up the great procession.

'Now then, Johnny!' said the neighbour, 'there's fine sights, surely!'

'Boo—oo, boo—oo!' said Johnny. 'Boo—boo—boo—booöo!'

The last elephant disappeared beyond the green, the strident strains of the band grew faint and more faint. Johnny stretched his neck.

'Nay, lad,' said Johnny's mother, 'they're gone—thou's seen t' last on 'em.'

But Johnny continued to gaze. When the last notes of the music had died away, and all the folk had gone back to their work or pleasure, he turned an inquiring eye on his mother. She, too, had returned to her wash-tub, and Johnny was alone. He heaved a deep sigh, and fell once more to smiling at the shadows as they danced in the grass.

THE PRICE OF CONFESSION

LEANING his chin on his hands, folded together over the blade of the hoe with which he had singled one turnip-plant from another since seven o'clock that morning, Dick Garth stood in the centre of the field, a motionless figure. It was within an hour of noon, and the sun was burning fiercely in a sky destitute of clouds; but there still lingered a bright dew-drop here and there on the dull green of the turnip leaves, and it was on one of these that Dick's eyes were fixed. He had gone up one row and down another with monotonous regularity for over four hours, and had paused more than once to rest upon his hoe, and stare vacantly at something immediately before him. After each of such reveries he had fallen to work again with renewed vigour, and now, as he slowly lifted his head and reversed the hoe in his hand, he made as if to lop away the next bunch of superfluous plants with its bright blade. But ere the sharp edge touched the tender stems, it was arrested. Dick looked across the field, attracted by the dismal note of a crow that had perched for a moment above the hedgerow. It swayed uncertainly over the topmost twigs of a tree which the lightning had blasted into barrenness in a previous summer—a dusky speck against the steely blue of the sky, and beneath it the ghostly white of the boughs and silvery grey of the trunk, down the centre of which ran one long streak of black.

Dick suddenly flung down the hoe. He faced towards the withered tree. 'I can't work, it's no good,' he said, and walked towards the hedgerow. The hoe lay where he had thrown it. He plunged his hands deep into his pockets, and hung his head. His feet, cased in their heavy boots, left deep impress in the light soil, a yard of brown earth and green leaf separating each print. But at the foot of the withered tree he stopped. The crow uttered a final note of sepulchral protest, and flew slowly across the next field. Dick watched it out of sight ere he sat down beneath the tree to rest his head on his hands and fall to his thoughts again.

All that morning, and all the day before, and for many days before that, there had been but one thought in Dick's mind. It was not so much a thought as an image—the image of a man sitting in the condemned cell at Cornchester Gaol, counting the hours as they went by, reckoning up every minute that remained ere the door should open to admit the hangman. Dick's imagination was slow, dull, not easily stirred; but the thought of Stephen Meadows, in that awful cell, woke it to acute perception. He put himself in Stephen's place, as he sat there under the tree. There were so many hours to live. Multiply the hours by sixty, and there were so many minutes. Multiply the minutes by sixty—there were so many seconds. But a second is a long time, and a minute—why, in two minutes and fifty seconds you can decide a horse-race! And yet how fast every second seemed to go!—the first crowded on the second, and the second on the third, and the third on the fourth, and now the fifty-ninth was lost in the sixtieth, and there was a whole minute gone. And the minutes went quickly, too, and after them the hours—but there was an awful slowness about their progress for all that, because there was something coming.

The sweat stood in great beads on Dick's forehead, as he lifted his face and looked about him. From the next field the crow called to him with dismal iteration. He shuddered as though a spirit had laid a spectral hand upon him, and again his mind set to work. He saw the hangman busy with his victim, the little procession making its way to the scaffold to the dull, monotonous clangour of the prison bell; he saw the central figure——

'I shall go mad!' said Dick, and rose to his feet. He turned towards the gate, leaving the hoe where it had fallen from his hands. Near the gate he saw his coat hanging on the hedge, where he had put it when the sun grew hot. He stared at it, and passed on unheeding. Down the narrow lane to the village he walked, his heavy tread leaving little puffs of dust in the sandy soil between the deep ruts. His hands were still deep in his pockets, and his chin rested on his breast. Now and then he muttered unintelligible words; now and then he looked from left to right, always with the air of a man who sees nothing. But he went forward steadily, until at last, where the lane turned into the village street, he came to a little cottage perched on the bank-side. He stood before the door, irresolute, wavering, for a time, but at last he mounted the freshly scoured steps and knocked timidly.

A girl's face looked out at him through a few inches of open doorway. Then her hand set the door wide open, and she beckoned him to enter, with a slight movement of her head. Dick followed her inside, and looked round him. There was a stick-fire crackling on the hearth, and over its cheerful blaze hung a great black pot, from the open top of which came a savoury smell. Near the fire sat an old woman, heavily shawled and wrapped, whose head nodded rhythmically, as if it beat time to some tune. She looked round at Dick, and smiled vacantly ere she turned again to the fire. The old grey head went on nodding—backward and forward, backward and forward.

'Now, Lucy,' said Dick.

He kept his eyes on the fire, and did not raise them to the girl's face. But something told him that her own eyes were red with weeping, and that her white cheeks bore witness to an exceeding sorrow. He moved his feet nervously, and his fingers plucked at the buttons on his waistcoat, but his eyes never shifted from the fire and the pot that swayed to the crackling flames.

'Now, Dick,' said the girl.

'Is there—have they heard—will aught be done?' he said.

'No,' she answered. 'It's all over—we've had word this morning from the lawyer—it's all been of no use, Dick.'

'They'll hang him high upon the gallows-tree!' piped the old woman. 'High, high, high—high up for the birds of the air to feast upon!—eh, dear, I can remember 'em hanging in chains—they was brave days, was them!'

'Hush, mother, hush!' said the girl fiercely.

The old woman began to whimper. The girl crossed over and touched her hand. She looked at Dick, and nodded towards the door. Dick went outside and waited. In a moment Lucy came to him, and they stood in the middle of the narrow lane. Dick looked at her for a second, and met her eyes. He turned away and stared at the ground.

'Dick,' she said presently, 'he'll die innocent. It was never in Stephen to kill anybody—I 'll stake my soul on his innocence. Oh, to think that he 'll die—and like that!—to-morrow morning! Dick—Dick—it 'll kill me!'

Dick's voice seemed far away to him when he spoke.

'You loved him true, Lucy?' he said.

'I love him with all my heart,' she answered firmly. 'And he knows it now. I wrote it to him, Dick—I thought there might be some comfort—oh, my poor lad, my poor lad!—what shall I do, Dick!'

With an effort that seemed to drive the life out of him Dick turned to her.

'Lucy!' he said.

She lifted her eyes to his. 'Dick!' she said. The white face that she looked at made her afraid. 'Dick!' she said again. 'Dick! What is it?'

The tongue in his mouth seemed suddenly turned into dry, cracking leather. He tried to move his lips—his teeth met and clicked. But with her eyes on him he made an effort and spoke.

'Lucy! it was me! it was me—not him—that did it! I couldn't rest—till—till——'

She stood staring at him a full minute before she stepped forward and laid her hand on his shoulder.

'You? It was you?' She drew back again —a sudden change came over her face; it grew cold, hard, pitiless, as she looked at the man cringing before her. She lifted her hands to her forehead, and seemed to smooth something away from her temples. 'I don't understand,' she said brokenly. 'I—I've thought a deal of late, and I'm not quite clear about——'

As she stood staring at him, the cold look in her eyes suddenly changed to one of acute perception. She sprang forward again, and gripped his arm with fingers that seemed to arrest him as with the implacable justice of the law. 'I know!' she cried. 'You mean that it was you —you, and not Stephen—not Stephen! Speak, speak, man—isn't that what you mean?'

He half-turned to gaze at her face, but shrank away again from the fierce regard of her eyes. 'Yes,' he said. 'It is what I mean.'

'How was it?' she said. Her breath came and went in quick gasps, her fingers still kept their strict hold of Dick's arm.

'It was an accident,' said Dick. 'I swear to

God it was. I'd no enmity against him. But when they fastened it on to Stephen I said naught —because I thought—I thought they'd put him out of the way, and I should have a chance with thee, lass! It was all for love of thee, Lucy.'

The girl's hand unclasped itself from Dick's arm. She hastened within the cottage, and came back tying the strings of her sun-bonnet under her chin, with fingers that trembled at every movement.

'Come,' she said, motioning to Dick. He looked at her wonderingly. 'Where?' he said.

'To Cornchester,' she answered.

'To Cornchester?'

He echoed the words in a dull, meaningless fashion. But suddenly their import burst upon him, and his face turned deathly pale, and the sweat flushed thick upon his forehead. He put out his hands, as if to keep some awful thing away. But on the instant the girl was at his side, and had seized both his hands in hers.

'Dick! Dick! For the dear Lord's sake, Dick, be strong! O Dick, don't have two murders on your soul—come with me and right him. Dick—if you love me—if you love me, Dick, give me back the man I love!'

She had drawn close to him as she pleaded, and suddenly she lifted her face to his and kissed him. At the touch of her lips Dick drew himself up—the tides of irresolute manhood came back to him strong and vigorous. He looked at her for a moment, and then held out his hand.

'Come, Lucy,' he said.

Hand-in-hand they went silently along the sunlit road. It was noon, and there was scarce a figure to be seen in the wide expanse of level land on either side the way. But at a turn of the highway there came in sight the red-roofed town, and high above it the round tower of the gaol, that seemed to frown menace upon the green earth that came up to its very foundations. With a quick consent their eyes turned to it at the same time. There was a sudden tremor in Dick's hand, but in a moment it was steady again. They went on—two lonely figures against the close-cropped hedgerows.

In the turnip-field lay Dick's hoe, its blade resting against the last plants that it had struck out. The sun that glinted upon its polished surface had withered the plants into premature death.

THE LAST LOOK ROUND

As the April sunshine stole into his room, Martin Summers awoke and looked about him with sleepy eyes. He sat up, and, leaning on his elbow, stared at the ceiling and the walls. The lath and plaster were falling from the ceiling, and there were unmistakable evidences of damp in the long streaks of discoloured wall-paper. His eyes wandered to the window, and rested on a wisp of straw that had been stuffed into the jagged opening left by a broken pane. Thence they turned to a curious examination of the room. The floor was bare concrete—there was neither mat nor carpet for bare feet to step upon; the walls were destitute of picture or ornament, save for a tattered Scripture text that hung from a nail above the mantelpiece. There were no hangings to the crazy bed, and beyond the bed there was no single piece of furniture in the room. Martin's clothes lay on the floor where he had thrown them the previous night.

'So this is the end of it all,' said Martin, and got out of bed. 'A fine end, truly! Land and money, money and land, house and home, home and house, all gone—and me a beggar. A fine end!'

He picked up his clothes and huddled them upon him with no more care than he would have displayed in dressing up a scarecrow. Pulling his coat on, he went down the stairs, his heavy boots waking dull echoes in the deserted house. He heard the scuttering of mice on the hearthstone of the kitchen as he passed through, and never turned his head to glance at them. Mechanically he walked to the door and took down a rough towel that hung there on a roller. From the window-ledge he picked up a bit of yellow soap, hard and dry. The door into the yard was open—he had not thought it worth the trouble of bolting when he went to bed the night before. He walked into the yard and washed himself at the pump. The cold spring water revived him, and he looked about him, drawing a long breath of satisfaction as he turned back to the house.

From a cupboard in the kitchen Martin Summers took a crust of bread and a bowl of milk. He sat down in the window-seat and lifted the bread to his mouth. 'The bread of bitterness!' he said, as his teeth met in the crust. And he laughed sneeringly, with a laughter that checked itself abruptly ere the full note came. The first mouthful seemed to choke him, and he made as if to put the bread down, but lifted it to his lips again instead, and munched steadily at it, swallowing every crumb with evident distaste and difficulty. Then he drank the milk at a draught, and looked at the empty bowl as if it were some curious specimen of pottery. He suddenly flung it from him with a turn of his wrist, and it hit the rusty bars of the fireless grate and smashed into small pieces with a harsh ring.

Martin laughed again, and rose to his feet. He stood irresolute for a moment ere he walked across the kitchen to the parlour door. But with the door once open and the empty parlour lying before him he hesitated no longer. He went in and walked round it, looking curiously at the bare boards, the blackened hearthstone, the marks on the walls where the pictures had hung. By the window he stopped, standing on one particular spot, where his mother's chair had always stood. There was a fine view of the garden and of the country beyond from that window—he looked at it now with eyes that saw naught of it. Presently he turned away, and began to explore the rest of the house. He, went from one room to another, upstairs and downstairs, and even into the cellars, by the stone steps that had been worn and hollowed by the feet of half a score generations of his ancestors. And at last he had visited every corner of the old house, and he came out at the front door and stood on the doorstep, shading his eyes from the sunlight as he looked about him.

In the paddock there were unmistakable evidences of the previous day's sale. The grass was strewn with straw, bits of rope, odds and ends; a well-defined circular track showed where the horse-ring had been set up; further away the ground was trampled into mud by the feet of sheep, cattle, and pigs. Under the trees still remained two or three old implements—a roller, a drill, a pair of harrows, sold for a shilling or two to some purchaser that repented his cheap bargain, and left his purchase unclaimed. Martin looked at these things as he marched across the paddock and into the wide meadow beyond.

'A fine end!' said he bitterly. 'Truly a fine end! Empty house, empty barn, empty stable. Once the house was full of plenishing and plenty—there was never stint nor hindrance to lad or lass within its doors. There were corn in the barn and horses in the stable—ay, better horses and more corn than in any farmstead of the wapentake. And now it's all gone—by heaven!' said Martin Summers, ''tis time I was gone too.'

And with that he began to think and remember. Twenty years had gone by since the old place came into his possession. There had been a Summers of Summerscote since the days of the first Charles—one of them had fought with honour at Marston Moor,—and each successive owner had added something of value to the place. For generations they had toiled and saved, rising early and working late, men and women—the men in the fields, the women in the dairy; and so they had come to be people of substance and of position. But wealthy as they were, there was never a Summers of Summerscote who felt himself entitled to play the fine gentleman until Martin's day. His father, it was true, had kept a good table, drunk his bottle of wine on a Sunday, and ridden to hounds twice a week in the season; but there his extravagance stopped. It was a mild extravagance, and Martin, as a lad, had shared in it. He had vowed that when he came into full lordship things should be different. He would have his fling, he would enjoy life. Life, he said, was meant to be lived—it was something better than a dull round of daily tasks, relieved by a visit to market, a day's hunting, and an occasional bottle of wine. He would live royally and enjoy himself—he would acquire a reputation as a good fellow and a generous host, and there should not be a sportsman in the Riding to compare with him.

When he came into possession of land and money he was twenty-two years of age, and had an appetite for pleasure that had been whetted more keenly by the repression which his father's presence had exercised upon him.

There was never a doubt in his mind as to the riches of the dead Summerses lasting out. He was not anxious, as his father and grandfather had been anxious, to leave wealth behind him. He had no desire to deny himself in order to leave money to a son. All that he wished was for years of pleasure. Time enough, he said to himself when he fairly realised that he was lord and master of Summerscote, to think about serious matters when he grew tired of life's joys. So he plunged into the whirl of life, and never gave a thought to the morrow.

For five years the old mother, sitting in her chair at the parlour window, with Bible and knitting ever at hand, watched her only child's life with a terrible anxiety. She besought and warned, and sometimes commanded; and to all that she said Martin turned a deaf ear. He was never unkind, never remiss in his attentions; he was sedulous in his regard to her personal comfort, but he would have his own way. The old woman in time refrained from entreating him, and betook herself to prayer. She strove to shut her eyes to what was going on. There were days and days whereon Martin never came near the land and his labourers—he was away in Cornchester, or York, or London, roystering and seeing life. She felt that the money which his father had helped to gather together, and to keep when gathered, was melting away, and she was powerless. And at last she died, and so there was no check on Martin, and his career went forward at a faster rate than ever. There were not wanting those who had known and respected his father to come to him with advice and warning as to the fate in store for him if he persisted in his mode of life. But to some Martin answered with a careless laugh, and to others with a sullen curse; and neither failed to warn his counsellors that it was of no use wasting words upon him. He was a prodigal from his birth.

All these things came back to Martin Summers as he walked about the land that April morning. The end had been long in coming, for there was much money, and the land was valuable; but it had come at last. He had known twenty years of reckless life, and now it was over. The land was his no longer; there was not a beast on its surface that he could call his own; the old house contained naught but the crazy bedstead and the broken potsherds on the hearth—every stick had been sold to satisfy the rapacious creditors, and he was a beggar. 'And more than a beggar,' he said to himself, 'for I am a friendless man. Of all the men that spent my money, that lived on me and flattered me, who is there that will give me my dinner? Not one. A fine end!'

All that morning he wandered up and down the fields, thinking bitterly of his own folly, but at noon he went back to the house and turned into the fold with purposeless steps. He felt that something lay before him, and yet he knew not what it was. The whinny of a horse roused him. He looked up, and saw, watching him from the half-open door of a stable, the old beast that had been put up last of all the night before, and had been knocked down for a handful of silver. Its purchaser had left it in the stable over night, and now it whinnied for food. Martin approached it. With his hands in his pockets he stood staring at this wreck of his fortunes—a gaunt mass of bones with rheumy eyes and swollen knees. There was a halter round its neck, and he laid hold of it and led the old horse across the fold. He threw wide the gate into the paddock, but as he turned the beast loose he took the halter from its head.

The old horse shambled into the paddock and began to crop feebly at the grass. Martin looked at it, and from its bony ribs his eyes turned to the rope in his hands. He turned, and walked back to the stable. It was cool and dark in there, but light enough to show him a stout beam that ran across the roof. He climbed up, and made fast the rope. Then he came down and paused —and went over to the door and shut out the sunlight.

CPSIA information can be obtained at www.ICGtesting.com
Printed in the USA
BVOW02s1321040216

435517BV00002B/13/P